Broken Sky

Part Nine

Chris Wooding

Cover and illustrations by Steve Kyte

SCHOLASTIC

Other books by Chris Wooding:
Crashing
Point Horror Unleashed: Catchman
Kerosene
Endgame

Look out for
The Haunting of Alaizabel Cray

Scholastic Children's Books,
Commonwealth House, 1-19 New Oxford Street,
London WC1A 1NU, UK
a division of Scholastic Ltd
London ~ New York ~ Toronto ~ Sydney ~ Auckland
Mexico City ~ New Delhi ~ Hong Kong

First published in the UK by Scholastic Ltd, 2001

Typeset by M Rules
Printed by The Bath Press, Bath.

10 9 8 7 6 5 4 3 2 1

Check out the

Broken Sky

website

www.homestead.com/gar_jenna

Broken Sky

MAU GRIST

FAL JUJA

KUIKARA

1

Twisted to Evil

The eastern coast of the Dominions was flat and barren. It was a natural progression; whereas the lands to the west got wetter and more heavily vegetated, the further east a traveller went, the less plant life he or she was liable to see. The plains of the central continent gave way to the empty steppes, where the hard, salty soil supported only grass and small shrubs, and no trees interrupted the vast bleakness where winds howled across the land. Towards the coast, the already unfriendly earth became downright hostile, and dissolved into rocky promontories and beaches of stone and shingle.

Beyond the beaches, there was only the endless sea, the barrier that had kept the people of the Dominions – and their counterparts in Kirin

Taq – from reaching out to explore their planet. The shallows spread out for several miles beneath the waves, a shelf of rock like a great skirt. Ships had plied these shallows for many years, for they were the most efficient and safe way of transporting large cargoes between the coastal cities. But where the shallows dropped into the abyssal depths known to sailors as Deepwater, there creatures waited that could swallow a ship whole, and almost invariably did so if any vessel was foolish enough to tempt them.

Many theories had been advanced as to why the creatures habitually attacked the ships. One was that the thumping of the mechanisms that drove the ship attracted them. Another was that the spirit-stone energy that their Pilots put out did the same. Some people thought they simply saw ships as a particularly large morsel of food; others that they resented any encroachment on their territory.

It didn't matter anymore. A way had been found, through the genius of the Machinists, to quell the Deepwater monsters. The Pulse Hammer worked. But like all things, its purpose could so easily be twisted to evil.

Two quiet days had passed. The Parakkan forces had mobilized as best they could. Even now, they were approaching the Machinists' Citadel, hundreds of miles to the west. There were no settlements on the coast of the steppes, but at their northern end, where they met the mountains, there were towns and more. Tusami City lay to the northwest. The Nomen hunted across the grasslands, unaware of anything beyond their own concerns. They had long since received Jedda's message, and ignored it. If the Deepwater creatures came, they would hide, as they always did, becoming ghostly, camouflaged figures against the wastes. The concerns of the rest of the land were not their concerns. They would play no part in the conflict to come.

Out at sea, something massive broke the water, long and serpentine, sliding into sight and then down again, beneath the waves.

When history looked back on this day, it would christen the Deepwater monster that first trod the land of the Dominions as the Mau Grist, meaning *first destroyer.* The Mau Grist was one of the smaller of the Deepwater creatures, only three

3

hundred metres from snout to tail. It was also one of the most irritable, hence its speedy arrival on the coast. The thumping of the Pulse Hammer was making it steadily angrier. The bigger creatures took more to persuade them to stir their bulk; it might be days or even weeks before those creatures that were a mile or more in size would set foot on the land. By that time, the Dominions would be no more anyway. The Mau Grist was quite capable of laying waste to a medium-sized city; and its kin were not far behind it.

There was no one present to witness the moment when the waves bulged and parted, and the Mau Grist rose from the shallows, foamy water draining from its back. Its body was long and lizard-like, supported by three short pairs of immense legs that ended in broad, webbed claws. The scales on its body were colourless and deathly pale, each the size of a shield, tinging towards a pearly blue in parts. Its muzzle was covered with a beaklike mask of bone, sharing as it did a common (and distant) ancestor with the wyverns of the mainland. Its eyes were white orbs within the pallid frame of its face. It looked like something recently dead, some zombie of the sea or the ghost of a monster; but it was very much alive, and enraged.

Its forefoot stamped down on the stony beach, punching a great hole into the yielding ground, and the first step was taken towards the destruction that was to follow.

There were few settlements north of Tusami City. The mountains that capped the northern end of the Dominions were not especially inhospitable in climate, but the difficulty in traversing the terrain meant that most settlers had chosen the more comfortable central plains. This did not deter some people, however, though most had an ulterior motive for choosing to put their roots down through bedrock rather than into soil. For some, it was the isolation they wanted; for others, the mountains provided something that the rest of the land could not, such as ores or plentiful wyvern-roosts.

If someone were to travel north from Tusami City, after many days they might come across a forested valley where the foliage was slowly reclaiming the shattered land, and shrubs and vines were beginning to clamber over the burned and scorched remains of a wyvern stud. And if they turned east then, and continued towards the rising sun for another day or so, they would eventually reach Master Uji's training academy.

Master Uji was a teacher of Pilots, and one renowned the breadth of the Dominions for his skills. He was younger than might be expected of one whose accomplishments were so widespread, for there were Pilots who had trained under him who worked in every corner of the Dominions. Short and stocky, he had a rude thatch of black hair that he kept in order with a black bandanna; his skin was weathered and tanned from a long forty-five winters in the mountains, and he wore simple shirts and trousers that fitted his muscular frame. He had chosen the mountains for the very reason that many shunned them; the difficult terrain provided an excellent training ground for his young pilots to drive ground vehicles.

Today, he stood in the doorway of his house, a

little way removed from the flaking metal vehicle bays and hangars that clustered together on a low plateau, sheltered by the surrounding mountains. The sun was beating down, a fine Dominion summer's morning. Yet he had been unable to shake a black feeling of dread ever since he woke up that day. And now, as he shaded his eyes and looked towards the source of the strange, slow pounding noise that had been getting steadily louder for ten minutes now, he became acutely aware of one of the biggest disadvantages of living in the mountains.

Nobody had been able to contact him to tell him of the second of the Deepwater monsters, Fal Juja: *cruel pincer*.

It was a nightmare of legs, claws and thick, lumpy plates of armour that overlapped along its back. It was as if some manic creator had thrown together the worst elements of a woodlouse, lobster and crab, and then magnified them into something that was probably a third of the height of Fane Aracq, the palace of the deposed Princess Aurin. Its dark eyes were buried deep inside the interlocking plates of its body, shadowy glints from which probing antennae poked forth, moving restlessly ahead of it. Its immense carapace was supported by twelve crablike legs, each one splitting into two separate, clawed feet. Four enormous, misshapen pincer arms waved in the air as it clambered over the mountain ridge into Uji's view; great, vicious things, encrusted with barnacles.

Fal Juja was a hole-dweller, spending much of its life asleep in caves at depths where the weight of the sea above would kill most creatures. But like the Mau Grist and many of its brethren, it had not forgotten its ancestors who had crawled on the land, and it retained special chambers inside its body that helped to equalize its internal pressure when it rose to the surface. It usually lived on a diet of krill and plankton, microscopic creatures that it sifted endlessly into its rudimentary mouth. Its armour and claws ensured that it won its fights with anything large enough to challenge it.

But it was that very armour that had led it to be among the forefront of the monsters that raced angrily to investigate the source of the pounding pulse that thumped at them steadily. For its shell acted as an amplifier, reverberating and echoing with every beat of the Pulse Hammer and making what was already an immensely distracting sound into something near unbearable.

Master Uji's irises shrank to pinpricks as he saw the size of the creature that crawled over the mountains and down towards the plateau, where his precious training academy lay, and where his apprentices were already fleeing in panic or trying to save some of the vehicles by driving them out of Fal Juja's path. This was going to be a bad day indeed.

All over the Dominions, the story was the same. More Deepwater creatures were reaching the coast every hour. Already, the easternmost settlements had been destroyed. The creatures were venting their anger on anything in their way – and in some cases, making a detour to attack villages – in much the same way as irate children might kick at anthills out of spite. At this rate, every permanent town or city in their path would be in ruins within days.

* * *

"*Two* of them are coming towards us?" Hochi cried. "Mauni's Eyes, *one* would have been enough."

"Hey, boss-man, I'm just reporting what the wyvern-scouts saw," said Gerdi. "Both of them are heading here. Tusami City has the good fortune to be in their path. With how many they've seen all over the coast, we're lucky it's only two. Guess these are the fastest of the bunch."

"Oh, I think we're in trouble now," Peliqua said.

*((**We can expect worse if the Citadel does not fall soon**))* came the voice of Iriqi in their heads, carrying with it a grey hue of doom.

"Yeah, thanks, Iriqi," Jaan said sarcastically. "We didn't need reminding."

The five of them stood on one of the great platforms that jutted out of the mountain-face above Tusami City like half-embedded discs. These streets ran all the way across the huge, rocky wall that the city beneath backed up against, diving in and out of the mountain in a network of tunnels. Not far away was the market that Kia had once disrupted, so long ago, by slaughtering a cohort of Guardsmen in revenge for her father's death. Some distance below, the hot, sweaty streets of Tusami City spread out at the foot of the mountains, a chaos of dark iron and huge industrial pipes. Magma derricks pumped ceaselessly up and down, huge pistons within towers of cross-hatched scaffold, providing power to the hundreds of thousands who lived in the Dominions' northernmost city.

So many people, thought Hochi. *And what can we do to save them?*

Already, an evacuation was taking place. Some were fleeing to the plains; many went for the tunnels that ran deep into the mountains. But most had chosen to stay and fight. For the warriors among them, it was a choice between facing the Deepwater monsters within a fortified city, or meeting them on a plain, defenceless. Common sense dictated that only the first option was acceptable to most.

And so the five stood and looked to the east, and tried to think of how the creatures could possibly be stopped. Two Dominion-folk, two

Kirins, and a Koth Taraan. Gerdi had missed Jaan and Iriqi's presence over the last year; he had seen them only occasionally, and then not for long. Jaan had taken up a post as a facilitator between the humans and the Koth Taraan, sharing as he did a deep bond with Iriqi – who had been appointed facilitator for its own people, after its peacemaking efforts with the Keriags. It seemed the halfbreed boy had at last found his place.

Gerdi glanced back at them. There was the hulking Koth Taraan, ten feet high at the shoulder, with its massive, armoured forearms and lower legs dwarfing the rest of its body, its tiny head dominated by two huge, teardrop-shaped black eyes. And Jaan, the halfbreed, his blocky, coffee-coloured face framed by thick ropes of hair around which were twined all kinds of ornaments, collars and strips of coloured cloth, his saffron eyes as alien as Iriqi's. Never had he seen a more unlikely pair.

Peliqua smiled at him, catching his gaze. Even in the face of disaster, she never lost her good humour. In only a few days, she looked much better than she had in captivity; and the reunion between her and her half-brother Jaan had done much to raise her already indomitable spirits.

And then there was Hochi. Calica had been gracious in accepting his apology, but he had still not faced Ryushi yet. But Calica . . . she understood. She knew what he had been going through. And now Elani had provided him with an answer to his musing about Tochaa's legacy – not necessarily the *right* one, if there was even an answer at all, but an answer nonetheless – he had reverted to his old self somewhat. Or perhaps it was because he had got Tochaa's pendant back. Elani had confided in Gerdi that she thought it was Tatterdemalion who put it in their cell, and that he had been the one who took it in the first place, but they chose not to mention this to Hochi and he didn't seem to care.

The tangles we go through, thought Gerdi with a sigh. *Macaan can't win. It would be such a waste. We're all too complicated to be allowed to die.*

His own philosophy startled him, and he shook

himself out of his reverie. Enough of that. Action was what was needed.

We hold them off here, he thought, and then wondered if they really could.

2

The Wide, Reflective Black

The Machinists' Citadel had become what was possibly the most well-defended place in either world since history began. Virtually every single member of Macaan's forces was stationed there, more than could easily fit inside the Citadel itself. They swarmed around the fens and moors in thick blots, building outposts, trenches, earthen barricades; moving vehicles and cannons into position. Wyverns raked the skies, their Riders in red, their long black braids streaming from the back of their full-face helmets and flapping round their armoured shoulders.

It was ridiculous overkill; there were perhaps twice the number of troops and equipment necessary to defend a fortress like the Citadel. But then, there was nowhere else for them to go now.

Most of the troops were unaware of the Pulse Hammer's existence. Those who had observed the ripple across the sky as it activated had not known what the cause was. Many had guessed that it was somehow linked to the sudden appearance of the Deepwater monsters; but as far as they knew, they were simply defending their King. They had no idea that his unhinged mind had, in its despair, settled on suicide; that he intended to take them and the Dominions with him.

Thousands had deserted from Macaan's troops over the last week. The Parakkan forces had poured from the Ley Warrens and spread all over the Dominions, overwhelming and unstoppable. Many conscripts, seeing Macaan's power become shaky, had switched sides. Many more – and these tended to be the diehard Guardsmen who were disillusioned with their leader – had left after they decided that the King had truly lost his mind. He had conceded the Dominions back to Parakka, he had even abandoned his *palace*, and withdrawn all his forces back to the Citadel.

But all the defenders in the land could not stop

the enemy within. And Macaan was surrounded by traitors.

In an abandoned storage room lay the discarded remnants of a machine that had, like so many others, once been the pride of some anonymous Machinist before it was superseded and scrapped. It was a huge device, modelled on the crystalline plants of Kirin Taq and intended to capture the rays of the sun and reflect them internally, thus creating a highly efficient and inexhaustible source of energy. Lying on the floor amid the debris was a curved, leaf-shaped reflector of highly polished silver alloy.

A claw broke the surface of the reflector, reaching out as if it were not a solid thing but a hole to be climbed out of. And then came a human hand, and an arm; and at once, eight figures came clambering through into the dim storeroom, crawling out of their own reflections.

Calica; Kia; Ryushi; Li'ain; Whist; Jedda; Elani; and lastly Tatterdemalion, whose power had brought them through the mirror and into the heart of the Citadel.

"I see you are all here, then," said a thin voice

from the shadows, and Corm stepped forward, his mechanical eyes sweeping over them all, and lingering just a little longer on his Princess before turning away to preserve her secret.

"Not quite," said Whist, and snapped the fingers of his ungloved hand. Blink appeared next to him, winking unobtrusively into existence before loping over to his master, who knelt down and rubbed his jowls and neck affectionately. "*Now* we are," he said.

Ten of them. Ten to try and destroy Macaan's plan for good and save their homeland. The assault forces that already approached the Citadel were nothing more than a grandoise diversion. Macaan thought there was no way in except through hundreds of guards and sentries – unless they used the very same method that *he* had used when he first conquered the unassailable fortress. His own tactic turned against him. But of course, that was impossible without the Jachyra; and the Jachyra, he believed, were his.

"There will be no creeping about now," said Corm. "The corridors are too busy for stealth. We must force our way through to the Pulse Hammer."

"'Bout time we got a straight fight," said Whist, casting a cocky grin at Calica. She ignored him.

"Couldn't you have got us nearer?" Kia said, giving Tatterdemalion a wary glance. To be with a Jachyra unnerved her considerably; she was at once repulsed and frightened by the ragged, mummified frame of the thing.

+++ **The Machinists were careful enough to remove any mirrors from any sensitive projects they were working on** +++ Tatterdemalion buzzed, without looking at her. +++ **They knew of the capabilities of the Jachyra. They did not want to be spied on any more than they had to be. But they could not remove every reflective surface from the Citadel. This is as close as we can get. We cannot step out of a mirror into the middle of a crowded room** +++

"Will you be coming with us?" asked Elani, sounding frankly terrified at the prospect.

+++ **If Macaan hears that either Corm or myself is alive, he will kill us with his trigger-stone. It is only because he thinks us dead that we remain the opposite** +++

"Is that a no?" said Kia.

19

Tatterdemalion paused. +++ **Macaan intends to kill the Jachyra anyway** +++ he said. +++ **He has nowhere to run now; he is cornered. He intends to take as much of the Dominions with him as he can. He will not spare us** +++

A short whine of feedback faded into the silence at the Jachyra's grim pronouncement. His telescopic eye whirred and retracted a little.

+++ **Every Jachyra is with you** +++

The assault, when it came, was swift, and unexpectedly savage. The Parakkan army was far greater in size than Macaan's spies had led him to believe. They had counted only the military camps, and overlooked the hundreds of towns, villages and settlements who, once liberated by Parakka, had pledged to fight alongside them to rid the Dominions of Macaan for good. The word had been spread that it was useless to defend their homes against the Deepwater creatures; only by taking the Citadel could they stop the advance of the monsters. And unlike their previous tyrant King, they trusted the word of Parakka.

The gross miscalculation of Macaan's spies meant that they had underestimated the number that they would be facing by a little over a third. Untrained warriors with inferior weapons, true; but they burned for revenge and retribution, and they would fight hard. Balancing them were the Koth Taraan, the gentle, hidden race finally roused to anger by Macaan, each one a miniature mountain towering over the heads of the others.

Kirins, Dominion-folk and Koth Taraan, fighting together; mukhili rose like islands from the army, howdahs brimming with desert nomads; pakpaks and horses and krel rode side by side with vast war machines. Wyverns circled the sky like crows, blackening the fine morning sky with their wings. Macaan's entire aerial force had been recalled to the defence of the Citadel, and Parakka had mustered everything they could to meet the challenge.

Two armies, of a size and variety never seen before.

The Parakkan force did not stop on its approach to regroup; it simply ploughed onward, closer and closer to the defensive barricades that were laid along the moors, and as if at some unseen signal, the battle began.

"Uh-oh," Gerdi said, as Fal Juja loomed briefly into sight in the lens of the spyglass, approaching along the line of the mountains.

"Uh-oh is right. You think you feel like helping out now?" Jaan replied snappishly.

"Oh, right. Sorry," Gerdi said, and quickly unrolled his spyglass – two magnifying balls of glass wrapped in a cone of leathery hide – before replacing it in his pack and applying himself to screwing small wires into the detonator box that sat by his feet.

Tusami City was a big place, but it was surprising how fast it pulled together in the face of the impending disaster. Most of the citizenry, lacking any chain of command, had started their own personal civil defence efforts, building huge barricades in the street, affixing spikes to rooftops, laying explosives alongside tall towers to cave them in on the monsters. People saw them and joined in, lending their shoulders and hands to the task. There was no real organization other than the common cause, but an incredible amount was done in a very short time.

And it was still not half enough.

The city guns opened up on the Mau Grist as soon as it slid into range. They were old, almost obsolete things, put there after Macaan first invaded the city and not used since then, except to fire a few brief potshots in retreat at the Parakkan forces when they came to reclaim the gateway to the mountains. Most of them missed even something as massive as the Mau Grist at the limits of their range, but as it got closer, they began to make more and more strikes. The creature flinched at each one, loosing roars of pain before shrugging them off and carrying on with redoubled fury.

But then the wind-sirens started up, howling across the city, as the mountain lookouts raised the alarm. Fal Juja was there, rearing out of a canyon that it had been following behind the sheltering peaks, closer than they had imagined it could get. There were no effective cannons to defend against something approaching Tusami

City from the mountain side, so all they could do was watch in terror as the immense, armoured thing advanced towards them.

"Get into position!" roared Hochi. Fal Juja had pulled back out of sight, and from where they were, down among the streets, they could only feel the massive movements of the creature above and behind them. The Mau Grist, its presence obscured by the high stone-and-metal buildings, had broken into a charge, its six legs stamping the ground as they carried its long, sinuous body towards the city. The city guns were powerless to hold it back; they stopped firing as their operators ran in terror to save their own lives.

Hochi and the others retreated from the hot, dirty street, heading back into the maze of alleyways that jinked and dived over and past each other. Hochi knew the city well, despite his long absence, and Gerdi knew it even better. They executed a series of turns and switchbacks before emerging into a kind of public stone gazebo that stood on the flat roof of a wide, low building. It provided a little shelter from the sun, and hid them well enough, but more importantly it gave them a view of the street that they had just primed with explosives.

They had just reached it when a great shout of alarm rose up from the city, and they looked up to see the crustacean face of Fal Juja peering over the lip of the mountain that backed on to Tusami City. Jaan's heart sank. It was only now that he realized what the Marginals back home had been talking about all these years, with their hoary old tales about sea creatures the size of a small town. As the dark, baleful eyes stared down at the city, he realized just how hopeless their situation was.

But worse was to come. Because there was no effective system of mass communication in Tusami City, it had been impossible to organize a concerted defence. This meant that most people made the best they could out of what they had. It was inevitable that people might tread on each other's plans; but no one could have imagined the scale of what was to come.

A mob of fifty concerned citizens had raided the city armoury and, knowing the direction Fal Juja was coming from, had decided to mount a drastic assault. They had set explosives all along the mountain ridge. Jaan's face, frozen in horror as Fal Juja loomed over the precipice, was suddenly awash in bright light as the ridge erupted in a wall of fire and smoke, blasting great geysers of stone powder high into the air. A deafening screech came from the creature as it disappeared among the great gobbets of billowing dust.

The blinding flare of Iriqi's alarm flashed through all of their heads, but it was Hochi who unleashed a savage oath. "Don't those idiots know there's people down below?" he cried. Small stones were peppering the gazebo roof now, tapping and cracking insistently and rapidly, thrown up by the explosion and descending at fearsome velocity. Larger boulders and thick slivers of rock were crashing down the sheer face of the cliff, smashing into the mountainside streets in an avalanche of grey dust and ricocheting off to land in the streets at the foot of the mountain. There was never much real danger of starting a landslide – the mountain face was solid rock – but the damage that the explosion did to the buildings beneath it was considerable.

This is only the beginning, Jaan said to himself, his saffron eyes ranging over the few dozen collapsed buildings.

But now the smoke cloud on the ridge was clearing, feathering at the edges and being torn into tatters by the summer breeze, carrying the acrid smell of the explosives over the city. For a few seconds, the whole city held its breath; but then the dark, lumpy shell of Fal Juja poked through the folds of the cloud, and thousands looked on in dismay as it raised itself up on its crab-legs and screeched in fury.

And then the ridge gave way.

It was not a landslide, not as such. There had evidently been someone with some skill in demolition who had been overseeing the placement of the explosives, however, for the shelf of rock that came tumbling down was a little too neat to be accidental. The very lip of the mountain had been weakened by the explosion, and the monster's great weight was enough to make it crumble. With a new screech, it toppled forward, accompanied by a tumultuous army of boulders that thundered down with it, and the city could only look on as the enormous body of Fal Juja crashed down the cliff face.

The destruction was immense. The flailing beast carved a furrow down the cliff as it fell, smashing buildings and streets beneath it. Those that it missed on its fall were destroyed by the boulders that charged recklessly with it. Most of those who lived on the cliff face had had the sense to retreat into the underground tunnels, where the majority of the city's population were now crammed; Peliqua hoped that everyone had made it in time.

Fal Juja hit bottom, and four of those in the stone gazebo staggered as the boom of the shockwave hit them. The fifth, Iriqi, did not.

It all seemed to happen in slow motion, and when the cataclysm was over, and the last boulder had stilled, all was silence. As the new uprising of dust settled into a foggy, murky blanket over the streets, the extent of the devastation was slowly unveiled for the city to see. The entire cliff community had been destroyed. Only a few pathetic half-walls and stony juts bore witness to the network of streets and buildings that had existed there moments ago. At the foot of the cliff, there was nothing standing; those constructions that had not been flattened by the impact had been buried under the boulders that came down in Fal Juja's wake.

Peliqua made a little "oh" noise.

The price was terrible. But the one thought on everyone's minds was: had it worked? Hochi didn't know whether to condemn whoever thought of it for their callousness or commend them on their genius. By sacrificing a section of the city, they hoped to stop Fal Juja destroying the whole of it. And it had been a hefty fall, even for a creature so big.

Had it worked?

And then the screech, bringing a black wash of dread from Iriqi, shot through with seams of maudlin blue disappointment. Fal Juja rose again, shucking off boulders from its armoured back, its crab-legs ratcheting to right itself. Its four great pincers raked the air and it screeched again from deep within its barnacle-encrusted shell.

Which was when the Mau Grist hit the city walls.

It piled into the iron construction at a charge, so enraged had it become by the guns that had harassed it. It would have been easy enough for a creature the size of the Mau Grist to simply climb over the barricade, but its mind was clouded with animal fury, both from the hurt it had received and because it was even closer now to the source of the maddening pulse that had drawn it in the first place. It dented the wall considerably, but it had reckoned without the tensile strength of what it was up against. Again and again the Mau Grist pounded at the barrier, damaging itself in its frenzy, until finally the obstacle bowed and buckled, and tore apart at its riveted seams. The creature roared in triumph as it slunk into the city, its massive legs knocking through brick and stone like they were not there, wading through buildings with impunity.

"He doesn't look happy," said Gerdi, rubbing his hand through the bright green thatch of his hair.

"He's gonna be even less happy when he reaches the street we've laid with explosives,"

Jaan pointed out, and indeed the creature was heading directly for their trap, it seemed. And uncomfortably close to where they stood beneath the gazebo, mere mice in comparison to its great size.

((You should get to a safer place)) said Iriqi. *((I can call you when the creature is in position))*

The Koth Taraan tended to be silent when there was more than just it and Jaan there, a silent, solid presence in the background. Today, it had been occupied with relaying the events of Tusami City to the Communion, the network of links that bound together the shared thoughts and memories of every Koth Taraan. As it had been watching the battle being fought at the Machinists' Citadel through the eyes of its kin, so they had been watching the destruction of Tusami City through its own. Now it spoke, to remind them that its race's method of speaking – which went directly to the brain without passing through the ears – meant that only *one* of them had to be in danger. They could pass out of shouting range and still hear it. Its outsize claws could not work the detonator's twist-switch – only the artists and sculptors of its race were dextrous enough for that – but its armoured body would provide it protection while it took the dangerous job of being the lookout.

"I'll stay too," said Jaan immediately.

"Don't be dumb," said Gerdi. "Iriqi's right. If that thing decides to go off course then there's no telling what—"

"Mauni's Eyes, *no*! Look!" Hochi cried, pointing across at the Mau Grist. Gerdi had not even finished his sentence before the massive creature had, indeed, changed direction and begun thrashing away towards another end of Tusami City. But it was not that that caused the fear on Hochi's face.

The creature, in its rage, was blundering straight for one of the magma derricks.

"Er . . . what's going to happen when it hits that big tower?" Peliqua asked innocently, seeing Hochi's look.

"I dunno," said Gerdi. "But you can bet it's not gonna be good."

Fal Juja screeched, smashing its way through the suburbs of Tusami City.

The Mau Grist careened into the metal lattice tower that housed the magma derrick.

And Tusami City's fate was sealed.

Like so many such things, nobody had considered it would happen until it did. When the Machinists had proposed the magma derricks several dozen years ago, as a way to power the growing metropolis of Tusami, they had included many failsafes and overrides to cope with almost any eventuality. After all, machinery was prone to break down over time, no matter how sophisticated it might be.

One thing that was not taken into consideration was the possibility that the derrick might be destroyed completely.

It was only natural, really. They lived in a world where the few things powerful enough to destroy a structure of that size were mainly owned by the Machinists' Guild anyway. It was too unlikely to plan for. And the Machinists' Guild were not renowned for their tendency to err on the side of caution. As long as they got paid, that was fine.

The magma derricks tapped the lava that ran beneath the mountains by a variety of pressure chambers, increasing and decreasing the density of the air to make the lava flow up from its deep channels to where its energy could be leached. When the magma derrick was toppled by the Mau Grist, it ruptured several of the pressure chambers beneath the earth, most of which were full of lava at the time.

The sudden and violent decompression of the chambers was explosive. The result was cataclysmic.

The initial blast annihilated both the Mau Grist and everything within a quarter of a mile, melting flesh and metal and stone alike in one raging furnace. From the epicentre, a low, rounded shockwave raced outwards, like a rapidly growing discus, gathering buildings and streets haphazardly together and crushing them into a broken jumble. A fountain of magma, hot enough to eat through any armour in the land, geysered upwards on a plume of shrieking yellow sulphur, and rained down on the city below.

There were three more magma derricks in

Tusami City. All of them would be destroyed by the blast, a chain reaction that would level the city. But the five standing in the gazebo would not see them go up. They were on the outskirts of the first blast, and in the three seconds that it took for the roaring shockwave to reach where they stood, time seemed to decelerate to a trickle.

Gerdi looked over his shoulder at Hochi, and the big man's eyes as he returned the gaze were kind and serene.

Jaan unconsciously grabbed his sister's hand and squeezed it tight. She smiled at him.

In the wide, reflective black of the Koth Taraan's almond-shaped eyes, the bellowing wall of destruction thundered towards them, and a hundred thousand of his kindred were with him as he waited to meet it.

Impact.

3

Hochi's Answer

"They're all over us! Come in! They're—"

The Guardsman's frantic call for help was silenced as three Jachyra tore him away from the intercom on the wall and ripped him to pieces. The corridor was awash with corpses, the floor slippery with new blood. The angular, mummified forms of the Jachyra stood everywhere, hunching over bodies or scanning for fresh prey. Less than a minute ago, the dark metal corridor had been populated by twenty Guardsmen; none remained.

"Don't be concerned about the intercoms," said Corm blithely, as he strode down the corridor, the hem of his greatcoat becoming wet with gore as it flapped about his booted ankles. "I've arranged to make it difficult for reinforcements to get here. Nevertheless, let's make this little coup as quick as possible, shall we?"

Ryushi's throat closed up at the stench and he threatened to gag. Elani's eyes were filled with tears, even though she had seen such horrors at first hand many times before. The others held a mixture of shock, disgust, sorrow and fear on their faces.

Corm halted while Tatterdemalion came over to him, accompanied by another Jachyra, who stood taller because of the unnaturally straight angle of his back.

+++ **It would be best if we dispersed now** +++ Tatterdemalion crackled through his circular voice-grille. +++ **These corridors split up to encircle the Pulse Hammer chamber. There are many routes in and out. We must not allow any Guardsmen to escape to raise the alarm** +++

+++ **My Jachyra will cover the exits and push inward** +++ said the taller one, and Corm recognized him as Vore, the new Chief, by the way he said "*My* Jachyra". Tatterdemalion turned to look at him, but whatever was in his mind did not show on his semi-mechanical face. Corm got the impression that the former Chief of the Jachyra was not happy with his subordinate taking his title, no matter what the circumstances. *He* was still the leader.

+++ **You will converge with us on the chamber** +++ Tatterdemalion said, pointedly reasserting his authority. +++ **And assault it on my command** +++

Vore was silent for a moment. The two of them would have glared at each other, if such a thing were possible.

+++ **Agreed** +++ he replied – conceding, but letting Tatterdemalion know his authority was not absolute any more. He had given up his post. That made he and Vore equals, in the latter's mind.

"Can we get *on* with it?" said Kia. "Those reinforcements *will* get here eventually."

Ryushi, who had been distracted searching for the source of the moist sound that he had been hearing since the slaughter had ended, saw Blink lapping at the warm blood that pooled at one corner of the corridor. He wrinkled his nose in disgust, and looked at Whist, who was wiping his mouth and grimacing as if he tasted something nasty.

"What, can *I* help it?" he asked Ryushi irritably, catching his glance.

The battle outside was fierce and desperate. The moors and fens resounded with the muted thump of military force-cannons, and the screech of wyverns overhead battled with the roar of war-machines as they ploughed over the soft earth, casting bolts into the milling mass of fighters that swarmed across the valleys and flats.

The Koth Taraan were as unstoppable as the Parakkans had expected them to be. Averaging ten feet high at the shoulder and nearly as broad, they were vast, squat behemoths whose thick exoskeletal plates could absorb the Guardsman's force-bolts, and whose massive, sabre-like claws could rip their armour apart like it was paper. They swept through Macaan's ground troops effortlessly, leaving nothing alive in their wake, taking out strategic points so that their more frail comrades could proceed towards the Citadel. Their linked minds made them a formidably co-ordinated force, and for such gentle, cultured creatures they were shockingly vicious.

It was strange, really. The Parakkan onlookers had noticed almost the exact instant when the Koth Taraan switched from a steady, measured force to a raging cyclone of claws. Something had angered them immensely. No longer were they fighting for political reasons – to rid themselves of the expansionist threat of Macaan – but because they were incensed by something. Of course, the onlookers had no way of knowing that their frenzy had coincided almost exactly with the explosion that had destroyed Tusami City, and taken one of their most valued kin with it.

But the Koth Taraan were few in number, and though they were an invaluable force for the Parakkan cause, they could not win the battle for their side.

High above the fray, a lone wyvern soared aloof. It was Araceil. No one but Ryushi could ride him now, but he would not leave his Bondmate, and so he circled above the battlefield, knowing all that Ryushi knew and relaying everything his pupilless amber eyes registered.

Never before had a battle of this scale been fought on Dominion soil. The forces of both sides stretched over the plunging landscape as far as the eye could see. Mukhili reared and crashed down on gun emplacements; Artillerists raked the sides of Parakkan war-machines from wyvern-back; Dominion-folk and Kirins sweated and bled and died side by side on the battlefield. A thousand heroic acts were counterbalanced by a thousand cowardices. In the horror of the war, men and women were made and killed, boys and girls lost their childhood or their lives, friendships and alliances were forged or torn apart in a single sweep of an axe or flail. Strangers saved each other's lives time and time again, with no thought to the colour of their skin or eyes or even their species. In the face of death, all of them were equal. And in the face of a common enemy, all of them were united.

This was Tochaa's Broken Sky. This was Hochi's answer. And somehow, from where he existed in a realm that allowed neither thought nor consciousness, he *knew* that, and was happy.

Ryushi threw up his defences a split-second before the force-bolts slammed into them, dampening the impact enough so that it did little more than make them stagger backwards. A moment later, the Guardsmen piled into them, coming from two sides of the T-junction, and sword met halberd as the two sides clashed.

Sweat flew freely from Calica's face as she fought to manoeuvre in the crowded corridor. Macaan had stuffed the veins of the Machinists' Citadel with Guardsmen, at least in the upper levels where the sensitive equipment was, and no more so than around the Pulse Hammer. He knew full well what Parakka would be after; they could only hope that he did not expect them to be able to infiltrate the Citadel without breaking down the outer walls.

Ryushi fought next to Calica, his sword slicing deep into the shoulder of an opponent before tearing free and parrying another blade. The combat was too close for him to dare unleash his power. Kia couldn't use hers because they were high up in the air with no earth around them. So here they were, hand to hand again, like it had always been.

Jedda and Kia defended one side; Calica and Ryushi the other. Whist sent his metal discs hurling down the corridors with lethal accuracy while Blink looked after Elani and Corm and Li'ain. Why had they let Elani come? Calica couldn't say. Without her Resonant powers, she was next to useless; but Ryushi would not allow himself to be separated from her again, and she would not be left behind in Gar Jenna.

But that was not the only reason. There was some purpose she had not yet served. Calica had not protested Ryushi's insistence that Elani come, because she, too, felt that the girl was somehow *necessary*. It was the strangest sensation, like being *guided*, as if one of Elani's precious connections that she was always theorizing about had suddenly tugged at them all. Elani had to come with them.

Why?

Kia blocked a blow aimed at her midriff and jabbed her staff hard into the Guardsman's face, rocking his helmeted head back for a follow-up strike to his exposed throat. Next to her, Jedda's scimitar had lost its sheen in the dim light, slicked by blood. Even in the midst of the battle, she found herself stealing a glance at the Rai'kel, and almost hating herself for doing so. He should have been out there riding a mukhili, but he fought with her instead. She watched his calm, unhurried slashes and parries out of the corner of her eye and felt an absurdly inappropriate sense of clarity. Here, as they were fighting for their lives, she suddenly knew something she had been suspecting for some time, and it invaded everything with its simple truth.

Oh, Ty. I loved you. I really did. But it was for the wrong reasons. It was because you were a part of my past, the only part of my childhood I could keep for myself. It's not like . . . not like. . .

Not like *this* is, she thought, and Jedda almost seemed to sense her mind then, and mid-stroke he turned his eyes to her, as if to say: *Do you mean that?*

Yes. Yes I do.

An unspoken and unheard conversation, carried on the medium of a simple glance, but in that moment the two of them had fallen in love.

A cry went up from the Guardsmen behind them, and then suddenly the Jachyra were there, sawing into the ranks of the enemy from the other side of the corridor, sandwiching them between their lethal finger-blades and the swords of Ryushi and Calica. The Guardsmen who were fighting Kia and Jedda saw this and ran, their boots rapping up the dim metal corridor, only for fresh shrieks to begin as they rounded the corner and came across another cohort of Jachyra.

The striplight's faint glow had turned red with a thick spray of gore, painting Tatterdemalion's face in bloody shadow as he stepped over the bodies to join the Parakkans and their companions.

+++ **We do not have much time** +++ he crackled. +++ **We must make haste to the chamber. My Jachyra have cleared the way** +++

"Alright!" Whist whooped, grinning. "Let's get on it!"

Ryushi cast a glance over his shoulder at the wild-haired boy with his skin-dyed tattooes crawling and spiralling over his naked upper body. He felt a moment of disgust, remembering Whist's callous attitude to killing. Could they really trust these people? Jachyra, Machinists, a mercenary like Whist, even—

Aurin? Their eyes met as if each knew the other had been thinking about them. She, Li'ain, was stronger now, less a spoiled child and more her own person, but just as achingly beautiful as before. Ryushi's mind flashed back to the times in his prison cell in Fane Aracq, when they had kissed even as they betrayed each other, she to destroy Base Usido and he to steal the heartstone and rob her power. And at that moment, he felt an almost physical need for her, to reignite the flame they once had, to—

Calica was watching them, anger in her olive-green eyes. He noticed her, and Li'ain broke his gaze and he felt ashamed and guilty all at once. Then Calica turned away, dismissing him without a word, and they headed off through the corpse-strewn corridors of the Machinists' Citadel to where the Pulse Hammer waited for them.

The death toll was terrible. Even though Parakka were relying first and foremost on Ryushi and the others to take down the Pulse Hammer, they still had Macaan's forces to deal with. Getting rid of the Deepwater monsters was only half of the problem. Macaan's power had to be smashed before the Dominions could be safe again. And so the Parakkans fought hard and viciously. They were fighting for their homes and families, and for their freedom, and for revenge.

But they were losing.

The Guardsmen were demoralized. They had lost faith in their leader, whose curious madness had brought them to this. They shared none of the unity of spirit that the Parakkan forces did. But they had three crucial advantages. Firstly, they were defending a fortress that was as near to impenetrable as it was possible to create. Secondly, they had state-of-the-art weaponry on their side. But most importantly, they had numbers. And no matter how strong the mukhili, how invincible the Koth Taraan, they could not do more than dent the mass force that was the entire army of Macaan.

Once the Guardsmen had been spread thinly across a whole continent; now they were gathered in a dense knot, and fighting because of the last thing that was left to them. Since infancy, they had been indoctrinated with a fanatical loyalty to their King; and even though they might not believe in him anymore, most would still defend him with their lives.

Who could have said how everything would have turned out if things had gone on the way they had? Perhaps Parakka, with their strength of will and spirit, would have doggedly beaten the Guardsmen down and saved the Dominions. Perhaps the Guardsmen would have routed the invading forces, not knowing that the only cause they were fighting for was their own deaths, to keep the Pulse Hammer operating for long enough to summon some of the *real* monsters of Deepwater, mile-long gargantua that would shatter the land as they fought and tussled with their enraged brethren who had also come to investigate the maddening pulse from the Citadel.

But two things happened then, two things that turned the tide of the battle. The first was heralded by an abrasive, distant noise, as of a rapid tapping, a *skittering* . . . and then, pouring over the fens, came the black, oily stain of the Keriags.

Thousands upon thousands in number, a sea of spider-legs and dark bodies and cruel, serrated spears.

The death of Iriqi had finally spurred the Queens into action, shaken them with the realization that they could not simply sit by, defending only the Ley Warrens. Their kin were being killed, the Old Brethren. For the Keriags and the Koth Taraan had sprung from the same ancient hive. And the hive protected its own. That was the way the Keriags thought; it was why they had assisted in Parakka's coup at Fane Aracq. And now it was the reason behind their decision to assist Parakka in the Dominions.

That was the first thing. The second was the arrival of Kuikara – *monstrous killer* – the largest of the Deepwater creatures to set foot on land so far.

Elani stood gingerly before the bloodied mess of a Guardsman who blocked her way, calculating where best to put her feet so that she would not have to touch it. Li'ain reached back to offer her a hand, but she shied away. She knew – in the way that she had of perceiving things that normal people missed – that Li'ain was Aurin. The others were gathered around the sliding metal door that was one of the three entrances to the Pulse Hammer room. The striplights flickered fitfully, illuminating the charnel house in rapid, bright flashes interspersed with near-absolute blackness. The Jachyra huddled close, ghoulish scarecrows that smelt of musty rags and still-wet blood. Ryushi, Whist, Kia, Jedda and Calica were nearest the door.

"They've locked it," said Calica. "Give me a moment." She went to work on the dials, slowly turning each one to its correct position, a soft hum surrounding her. Letting them "remember" their place in the sequence.

+++ **They will be waiting on the other side** +++ Tatterdemalion said, amid a low feedback whine.

"I'll cover you," said Ryushi. He had almost forgotten that the Jachyra were his mortal enemies in the heat of battle. "You guys get inside. El, stay out here until it's safe. Li'ain, watch her."

"I will," she said. Elani made a distasteful face, but didn't say anything.

"Can you get Vore to go in through the other door at the same time?" Kia asked.

+++ **I will do so** +++ Tatterdemalion replied.

"A word of warning," said Corm softly, from behind them. "Do not destroy the Pulse Hammer. There's no telling what will happen if you rupture any of the power sources."

"So we capture it and reverse it, right?" said Ryushi.

"Theoretically," Corm replied.

"Why do I not like that word?" Whist asked himself.

"Because it's too long for you to spell," Calica observed acidly.

"Touché," said Whist. "Still sore 'cause I hamstrung your man back in Kirin Taq?"

Calica rounded on him, but Ryushi held out an arm to stop her. "I haven't forgotten that one, Whist. I never trusted you, and I don't now. But you pull anything on us this time, and I promise you I'll spend the rest of my life hunting you down."

Whist examined the fingernails on his ungloved hand, pretending to be preoccupied.

He looked up after a moment. "Sorry, what'd you say? You were *threatenin'* me?" Blink growled from where he sat at his master's feet.

"Kids, can we save this till later?" Kia snapped. "Just get in there and shut up."

Ryushi cast one more venomous glance at Whist, then turned back to Calica. "You got the lock?"

"Done."

"You?" he asked the former Chief of the Jachyra.

+++ **Vore is standing by** +++

Ryushi shrugged. "Let's do it," he said, and hit the palm-stud.

The Guardsmen inside the room opened up the second that the door hissed open. Ryushi jumped into the room, his arms crossed in front of his face in an X as he threw up his defences. The salvo pounded against the barrier, pushing him back; he planted his feet and leaned into it. The number of force-bolts that battered him was overwhelming, relentless; even with his power, he knew that he could not hold out for more than a few dozen seconds.

But that was all that was needed. From behind his shield, the Jachyra poured in, led by Tatterdemalion, and as they leaped out to either side with the inhuman speed of their kind, the Guardsmen turned their aim away from Ryushi and tried frantically to pin down the lethal killers before they could reach the place where the defenders hid, behind the banks of machinery that circled the vast, endlessly high shaft of the Pulse Hammer.

And now, just as the defenders had decided that the assault was only coming from one of the three entrances and had turned to concentrate their fire, Vore's half of the Jachyra swarmed in. They had received word of the lock code from Tatterdemalion, and they struck on his command. Suddenly divided, with too many targets, the Guardsmen were lost. Their only hope in defeating the Jachyra lay in killing them as they came through the narrow doorways; and that chance had been missed now. In the open space of the Pulse Hammer shaft, the creatures had room to manoeuvre, and their frightening speed meant that it was virtually impossible to hit them as they advanced.

The interior of the Pulse Hammer chamber was a treacherous battleground. Circular in shape, floor level was a mass of grilles, shallow staircases and platforms that got higher as they wound closer to the Pulse Hammer itself. Overhead, a spiderweb of gantries and walkways lunged across the shaft to maintenance points on the device itself, along which Guardsmen were running and firing. Every corner provided an ambush point; no place was completely safe. And there, presiding over the mayhem, was the object of their conflict; a great black obelisk of metal, stretching up the massive shaft, with four smaller obelisks at each corner and the great round generator pods in between. It thrummed with energy, diodes and tiny lights flickering on its skin, switches and tiny pistons moving faster than the eye could follow. An enormous, dim giant in the half-light, watching the tiny, insignificant people in its shadow fighting to decide who would control it.

Calica leaped over a low bank of machinery, swiping down with her katana and feeling the jolt in her arm as it cut home, landing in a roll and coming up into a crouch. She pulled her blade free of the Guardsman's throat and let him slump from where he had been hiding, pressing her back against the cold metal of an operating station. She was exhausted, her body aching from being constantly on edge. The battle had been short but intensely fierce. All around her, the Jachyra were like piranhas in a feeding frenzy. The massacre was sickening; the Guardsmen didn't stand a chance. Even the ones who ran across the gantries overhead were being hunted down and thrown over the sides. The air thumped and warped with force-bolts; the echoes from the immense, hollow shaft made every shot sound like three. She barely dared move from the shelter she had gained.

Someone dropped from above, vaulting over the operating station that she leaned against, and she yelped in fright and brought her katana around. Her hand was grabbed in mid-swipe, and in the moment's pause she saw who it was.

"Kia," she breathed, lowering her blade. "Don't *do* that."

"Some fun, huh?" Kia grinned, echoing

exactly the words of her brother when he and Calica had been infiltrating the Machinists' Citadel for the first time. "You ready to go out there again?"

Calica looked less than enthusiastic. "Sure," she said.

"Three . . . two . . . *go!*"

They broke out on either side of the operating station, running low, heading towards the control panel that sat near the centre of the concentric circles of machinery banks that surrounded the Pulse Hammer.

And the sound stopped.

Calica exchanged a puzzled glance with Kia. The din of the battle had suddenly faded, echoing away up the shaft into silence.

Jedda appeared next to them, dodging between the banks of machines. None of them dared raise their heads to look out. The silence was unnerving.

"I think that the last of the Guardsmen has been slain," the Rai'kel suggested, his scimitar held ready.

"*Ryushi?*" Kia called. "You out there?"

Calica pointed over at something, tugging Kia's

sleeve. The door that they had entered through was shut.

"Something is wrong," said Jedda.

"Sis?" came Ryushi's voice. "Sis, we got trouble. Take a look."

The three of them peered out of their cover, and saw Ryushi there, with Whist next to him, surveying the scene around them with an expression of uncertainty on his face. She stood up, and the others with her, and Kia caught her breath as she saw what he meant.

From where they stood, in the midst of the waist-high rows of machinery that operated and monitored the Pulse Hammer, they could see perhaps half of the room, but that was enough to tell them what was going on. The Guardsmen had indeed all been killed, faster than they would have believed possible; if there were any left, then they were few enough not to matter. But lying amid the blood-slicked black of the Guardsmen were the Jachyra, too. Not just one or two that might have been hit by force-bolts. All of them.

Struck by a sudden horror, Kia looked back at

the doorways through which they had entered. They were both shut, and the corridor that provided the third entrance had sealed itself off. She, Ryushi, Jedda, Calica, Whist and Blink; six living things left in the whole, vast echoing shaft. Elani, Li'ain and Corm outside.

What about them? What about Elani!

"Will someone tell me what's goin' on?" Whist asked, his voice breaking the quiet.

A soft, sinister chuckle floated to their ears, seeming to come from the walls of the chamber.

"Macaan," Kia breathed.

They cast around frantically for the source of the sound. The multi-levelled floor that surrounded the Pulse Hammer, lifts and stairs and unfathomable machinery; the metal gantries and walkways that ran across the darkness high above their heads. Nothing.

"Oh, children," came the King's voice, and he stepped out of the shadows that nestled at the foot of the immense Pulse Hammer array. "You really have caused me an intolerable amount of trouble."

Time seemed to slow as they looked at him,

there in the centre of the concentric circles of machinery banks. Standing on different levels, each lower than him, they seemed from above like planets in the orbit of a sun. All this time, ever since they had been thrown into this war, Kia and Ryushi and Calica had fought this man's forces, battled through obstacles that this man had erected, had their friends and family killed by *this* man, endured the unendurable because of *him* . . . and now he was here, the fulcrum of it all, the faceless King who had been their ultimate target since they had begun this journey.

He stood tall, his white hair immaculate as it fell about his shoulders, his perfect lips set in an arrogant half-smirk as he regarded the intruders with eyes paler than new ice on a pond. He wore a purple military uniform, severely trimmed in deep crimson with a stiff collar, black boots and a fine sword hanging from his belt. The dark indigo ellipse of his trigger-stone showed through the unblemished white of his forehead, a faint glow deep within its heart that was diminishing rapidly to nothing.

"You killed 'em," said Whist, looking round at the bodies of the Jachyra. "I kinda liked that Tatterdemalion guy."

"Be silent, you painted fool," the King said calmly. "Their deaths were a mercy to them. They had served their purpose."

"You *knew*?" Calica exclaimed.

"Of course I knew. I knew that they would betray me as soon as they thought it was safe to do so. I knew it would take little to turn them over to your side once the tide went against me," he smiled slowly.

He alighted his cold gaze on Ryushi. Ryushi met it, not daring to break it off. *He doesn't know it was Aurin behind it all. He still thinks she's dead.*

"But now their time is done, as it is for my other aides. I need them no longer. I have *you*," Macaan finished, and the room was suddenly filled with blazing, blinding light, which erupted outwards and then gathered in on itself as if sucked through a tiny hole.

The light faded, and where Kia, the King and the others had once stood, there was now no one.

Only the silent corpses of the slain remained amid the cool shadows and the heady smell of oil and blood.

And in a corner, there lay the still body of Tatterdemalion, his tormented existence ended at last, unlamented and forgotten.

4

The Balance Between the Worlds

It was Osaka Stud. They were standing in the central clearing of their childhood home, a soft breeze stirring puffs of dust from the hard-packed earth beneath their soles. It was a perfect summer's day, and the sun rode high above the forested sides of the valley, blazing down on the red metal rooftops of the buildings beneath: the low, round hatchery, its furnace rumbling as it incubated wyvern eggs within; the vast, wheel-shaped stables, with its hub, eight spokes and outer rim; the family house and its wyvern-scale roof; the grain silos, the vehicle bay, the perimeter fence. Everything was as it had been before the attack. Before their lives had been torn apart and stitched back together again by war.

"Wh . . . what is this?" said Calica.

"This?" Ryushi said, his voice dead. "This is home."

The four of them stood together: Ryushi, Kia, Jedda and Calica. A few metres away was Macaan, his oddly androgynous features serene.

"Ah, now where did that boy and his dog go?" he said. "No doubt they winked out before I could capture them. Resourceful thing, isn't he?" He drew himself up. "Still, he is nothing to me. Your friends may live or die, rot or prosper for all I care. We have business to conduct."

"Oh, we do?" said Ryushi, and suddenly threw out his arm, unleashing a terrific bolt of force that raced through the air between them, raising twin fins of dust from the ground with the shock of its passing.

"Don't be ridiculous," Macaan said idly, raising one hand. The force-bolt shrivelled and died, turning into a small acorn that the King caught in his hand. "Here," he said, casually tossing it back to them. It sailed slowly through the air, touched the ground and exploded, throwing out all the energy of Ryushi's initial attack. He threw up his defences, but not fast enough to prevent them all being blown off their feet and going sprawling and thumping to the ground.

They picked themselves and each other up, glaring at the King with a mixture of fear and hatred as he laughed softly to himself.

"You can't hurt me here, you little fools. This is *my* realm. Here, I can do whatever I like. I can twist the world in whichever way I see fit." He stepped up to Ryushi, cupping his hand roughly under the Parakkan's chin and pulling his face up so that they were eye-to-eye. "I can do *anything*," he hissed.

Kia's gaze was cold. "Where is this place?"

Macaan turned his head to her, still holding Ryushi by the chin. He seemed paralysed, his body limp, unable to lash out at the man before him. "This? This is Netherfane, my dear. This is my home."

"Netherfane," Calica said in disbelief. "This isn't Netherfane. We would have gone mad just seeing it."

"Oh, we can't have *that*," said the King, mock-pleasantly, as if speaking to an infant. "Where would be the fun then? There's no point in having you all die of shock. So I've protected you. I've created some familiar surroundings for you all. So I have time to make you *suffer*." He forced the last word through the grate of his teeth, throwing Ryushi away from him. Calica and Kia both ran to him as he slumped back to the sun-baked dirt again.

Calica looked at him poisonously from where she crouched by the fallen Ryushi, helping him back up. "You're lying," she said. "Your whole power structure was based on lies, and you won't stop now. Netherfane isn't your home. I don't know where you've brought us, but it's not—"

"It *is*, Calica," Kia said softly, pulling her up short. "I don't know how I know, but . . . it just *is*. I've *seen* it, remember? Not protected, like we are now. I saw it. And this . . . this feels the same."

Macaan gave a languid smile, his beautiful features curving elegantly. "The girl is correct, of course. The time for bluffing is over. Netherfane was my home as I grew, as much as Fane Aracq was. I did have something of a split childhood, you see. Juggling my roles as a young King of Kirin Taq, and learning to be—"

"A Deliverer," Ryushi finished for him, a thin trickle of blood running from the side of his mouth. "You're a *Deliverer*."

"Oh yes," Macaan said. "And here in Netherfane, that makes me a *god*!"

There was a beat of cold silence.

"You see, it was just you that I wanted, Ryushi," Macaan said, his pale eyes ghosting over the faces of the four who stood before him. Kia had unconsciously moved closer to Jedda, whose body was set in a ready stance, as if to react to an attack. "Lost kingdoms can be recovered, you realize. Kirin Taq can still be mine, and the Deepwater creatures cannot touch me here."

Ryushi felt a jolt of understanding at his words. Macaan *wasn't* intent on suicide; it just appeared that way. Mad, yes; insane with loss, possibly. But he did not intend to be around when the Dominions were crushed. His plan was to get Ryushi in revenge for Aurin. And when that was over, the King wouldn't be done. His threat would still be very real in both the worlds. He would be back.

"I am very aware of the part you and your sister

played in Parakka's rise in power. Surely it must be something genetic. Your cursed father and mother were the same."

Kia jerked forward, ready to attack him for slighting their mother, but Jedda put an arm out before her to stop her.

"You can't fight him yet," he said quietly. "It is better to wait."

"You can't fight me at *all*," Macaan corrected, looking past them to the gently stirring leaves of the trees that carpeted the sides of the valley. "You are here as witnesses to the final act of the play that I began. Do you know what a pyrrhic victory is, you pathetic creatures?"

"It's when you appear to win," said Calica. "But you really lose."

"Close enough," said Macaan. "It is a situation where the winner's losses are as great as the loser's." He tipped his hand in a casual gesture. "It appears that I have lost. I knew that from the moment you stormed Fane Aracq and killed my daughter." His voice was dangerously calm. "My theorists tell me that there is a high probability that the creatures of Deepwater, in their agitated state, will begin to attack each other once the Pulse Hammer is disabled. Most likely your land will be destroyed in the process. I will make certain *your* losses equal mine."

Ryushi kept silent. The King still believed Aurin was dead. He could not conceive of Parakka storming Fane Aracq and *not* killing her. And if she had escaped, why hadn't she come back to him?

Aurin. Li'ain. Where are you?

"So, to begin," the King said, and again Ryushi felt the awful paralysis suddenly seize him, as if his heart had suddenly begun pumping stone around his veins, freezing him from his centre to his extremities. The King walked over to him, and while Kia and Calica tried to lunge in interception, none of them could move. Jedda watched him carefully with feral eyes.

The King reached out and laid his finger on the small, red diamond on Ryushi's forehead; his Bonding-stone. He leaned close, until his mouth was almost touching Ryushi's ear. "Really, child," he said. "You should know that being Bonded is a great responsibility."

There was a moment of shattering light, and Ryushi screamed. The invisible link between him and Araceil seared as if scorched, and his brain burned like fire. And then, slowly, the fire died. The unearthly pain receded, retreating like a tide, leaving his disorientated senses howling with the aftershock . . . and gradually that, too, smoothed to nothing.

"What are you *doing* to him?" Kia shrieked, straining against the invisible bonds that chained her to the dusty floor.

"I'm setting up the game," said Macaan. "We can't play the game without Araceil, can we?"

And there he was. Standing next to the King, towering over him, amber eyes bright within the protective bone mask of his face, his four wings folded. Araceil.

"Leave him out of it," Ryushi grated, from where he lay curled up on the floor, his head in his hands. Slowly, ignoring the aching in his body, he got to his feet. His eyes were haggard and bloodshot. "It's me you want, isn't it? It's me who killed your precious daughter, the murdering little tyrant. *I* killed her, with *this* sword." He pulled the blade free from its scabbard and held it before him, levelling it at Macaan. His paralysis had disappeared in an eyeblink, but he knew it was only because the King had allowed it to be so. The dazzling sun, high overhead, shone down the length of the sword. "Like I'll kill you," he said. "For what you did to my father."

Macaan gave a surprised laugh of genuine amusement. "Oh, your anger is much misplaced, my warrior boy. I didn't do *anything* to your father. It's touching to know that we think along the same lines, however. I have someone who you'll be *very* interested in meeting." He nodded at something past them, and the four of them turned around to face the newcomer.

Takami.

"Corm! What has happened? Corm?" Li'ain's eyes sheened with tears of fright and worry as she cradled the Machinist in her arms. Elani fiddled with the door dials, looking anxiously each way up the corridor.

The Machinist's eyes had never closed – it was impossible, for they were mechanisms and did not have lids – but the near-constant chittering as they focused and compensated for changes in the light had gone quiet as the tall figure had slumped to the floor, the rubbery folds of his greatcoat collapsing. Li'ain had caught him, slowing his fall to the ground, and now she supported his shoulders while she patted the fleshy side of his face uselessly. All the years she had spent with him, all the time he had been her aide . . . she had become so used to the constant tick and tap of the switches and ratchets that kept his Augmentations working, that she had ceased to notice them any more. It was only now they had quietened that she was struck by the terrible silence.

It was silent inside the Pulse Hammer chamber also, beyond the door. The frantic thumps and cries of battle had stilled.

"Corm! *Wake up!*"

"He's dead, Aurin," Elani murmured.

Li'ain snapped a glance at her, realizing the girl had called her by her true name.

"Wasn't hard to tell," Elani said, shrugging.

"Can't you—" she began, but then suddenly Corm jerked in her arms, and a feeble chattering started up again, ebbing and flowing faster and slower.

"Corm!" she said, switching her attention back to him. "You're alive!"

"Reserve power," he rasped. "Tried to . . . bypass Macaan's implants long ago . . . Never knew . . . if it would work. . ." He hitched a breath. "It hasn't. . ."

"No, you—"

"Listen . . . Macaan has . . . used his trigger-stone. . . All the implanted . . . his generals . . . the Jachyra . . . they're dead. . ."

"Tatterdemalion?" Li'ain asked.

Corm nodded. Wearily, he lifted his hand to his face, and tapped a slow sequence of numbers on the tiny studs that were part of his metal cheek.

"What are you doing?" she asked. He ignored her. Elani knelt down next to the dying Machinist, having abandoned her efforts to get into the Pulse Hammer room. Corm was fading fast . . . the speed of the chatter of his mechanisms was winding down again.

"Corm?" Li'ain pleaded. "What are you—"

"Shut *up* and let him get on with it!" Elani

hissed, grabbing her wrist. "Can't you see he's running out of time?"

Li'ain fell silent, a former Princess chastened by a child's words. Corm was hoarsely muttering to himself, talking on his communicator, too quiet to be heard by them. After a short time, he sighed.

"My communicator . . . has died. . ." he gasped. "I failed you, my lady."

"No," she whispered, holding him close, gathering his tall, half-mechanical frame into her arms. "No, you were the most loyal of all."

A faint smile touched his lips, and then the ticking and tapping of his artificially sustained life finally faded to nothing, and he went limp. Silent tears fell from Li'ain's fine cheekbones, dripping on to the high collar of the Machinist's greatcoat. Elani watched her without a word.

After a moment, Li'ain brushed her long black hair behind her shoulder, wiped her eyes savagely and straightened. "He has Ryushi," she said. "My father has him. I know it."

"*How* do you know?" said Elani.

"It's the only answer. They're in Netherfane."

"Netherfane?" Elani exclaimed in surprise.

Li'ain fixed her with a steady gaze, cold and clear, a remnant of the Princess she once had been.

"I'm the only one who can stand against him," she said. "Take me there."

"I can't *do* it," said Elani. "I . . . I'm not a Resonant any more. I couldn't do it even when I was. We can't go to Netherfane. If it's anything like the Deliverers told Calica it was, we'd go nuts anyway just by being there."

"Listen to me," said Li'ain, crouching down so that her face was level with Elani's. "There has to be a way. My father is a Deliverer. He was taken as an infant, like they all were. But when he found out about his parents . . . *my* grandparents . . . when they were taken by the disease that took my mother, he gave it up to be King. I don't know how, but he turned his back on them. I thought nobody ever left the Deliverers but . . . but he did."

"They say that even the Deliverers go mad in Netherfane," Elani said. "Slowly, but it happens. That's why they are like they are. Isn't that why Macaan is—"

"I don't know," Li'ain said. "I don't know. But Elani, he has *powers*. You know what the Deliverers can do? They can choose the power of a spirit-stone, Elani. They can alter what's inside it, the minerals it contains, to give it that certain resonance that allows it to affect a substance. But they're forbidden to use their powers for themselves. It's part of their creed, just like they can't speak outside of their city. All of them are equal, so as to keep the balance between the worlds. That's their purpose, it's why they exist." She took a breath. "But my father broke those rules. He created stones for himself, and implanted them himself. People thought you had to be an infant to receive stones, but it's not true. It's just that Deliverers won't do it. They believe that the stone should shape the person. A blacksmith will become a blacksmith, with a blacksmith's outlook and personality. It's their way of regulating us. The *pah'nu'kah*. They mete out the gifts of the Flow, but it's all done within the framework of a balance. By the time we're old enough to talk, they think we're too set in our ways to change."

Elani was amazed, her face lit in childlike wonder. "I've . . . I've been thinking about all this for years now . . . and you knew all along? You *know* about the relationship between the worlds?"

"I know a little," Li'ain said, her blue eyes fixed on Elani's. "Nobody knows it all. Nobody will ever know it all. That's not the point. Elani, they don't have a hope against him. Not with the stones he has. Only I can stop him . . . and even then I . . . I may not be able to beat him. Not in Netherfane."

"I can't," Elani said. "I lost my powers . . . I told you!"

~you can, Resonant child~ came a deep, guttural gurgle from down the dim corridor. *~i will see to that~*

Chiro sat curled up in a service duct, his thin back resting against a rack of warm pipes. He had been here ever since he had been ordered to deliver the cortex key to Macaan's men. They had let him go, and he had returned to his familiar warren of service tunnels, neglecting his maintenance duties. Just hiding.

It was not the action of a machine. It made no sense that he should be engaged in such a wasteful and fruitless pursuit. But he did it anyway.

It hadn't felt right. Machines weren't supposed to feel anything at all; *Breed* weren't supposed to feel anything at all. But he'd *known*, when he received that order from the Master Machinist, that he was being given an illogical command. He had known that Okre Jey would only order him to give up the cortex key and betray his companions if he was being coerced in some way.

It wasn't his choice. He had been given an order, one that superseded the order given by Corm. He had to follow it.

And betray Quain.

He had memories of Quain. Quain had known him ever since the vats. Chiro could not recall the first time he had seen the Machinist, but he remembered the good feeling he got whenever he had an errand or a task to perform for him. Quain was kind. Most Machinists treated Breed much as they would treat the ur-Lan – as if they were less than nothing, merely cogs in a machine.

As it should be, he thought. But he could not dispel the horrible, empty feeling inside. He had betrayed one of the only people who had ever treated him well. And he saw on Quain's face, in the moment they took him away, an understanding and acceptance of what Chiro was. One who had to follow orders. One who could not help himself.

Machines did not regret. They did not feel sorrow. And they did not hold on to the past.

But he was not a machine. Not entirely. And his lack of control over his mental functions both frightened and frustrated him.

His communicator buzzed and crackled, and a weak signal suddenly spluttered into life, accompanied by an identifying code that marked the sender as Corm. Unlike most other Machinists, he only sent his identity when he chose. Chiro showed no reaction as the message began, his blank metal mask-face as still as ever, the dark lenses of his eyes flat.

"Chiro. Chiro. Acknowledge."

"Chiro here. Your signal is weak. Retransmit?"

"I'm dying, Chiro. This is my last order. The

Master Machinist is dead by now. You . . . *kkst*
rtex key a*kkst*able the Pulse Hammer. I am the
hi*kkst*ing Machin*kkkkkkst* here. Act in the
Guild's best in*kkkst*st. You mus*kkkkkkkst*—"

The signal faded and died.

Chiro sat alone, surrounded by the hum and warmth of the Citadel. An incomplete order. He thought he knew what Corm was asking of him, but only on the basis of guesswork and intuition. Neither were infallible.

He knew what he ought to do. He knew what was best for the Guild. But he had no evidence that the Master Machinist was dead, even though he thought he probably was. And until he knew for sure, protocol demanded that *his* order stood. Okre Jey was of a higher rank than Corm. Corm had no right to overrule him.

His orders from Okre Jey had been to deliver the cortex key to Macaan's men. He had done that, so he automatically reverted to his usual duties: to look after the welfare and maintenance of the Pulse Hammer. If he followed those orders, he was certain that the Citadel would eventually be destroyed. In that case, the Pulse Hammer would be destroyed with it. His orders contradicted themselves.

He could jump through hoops of logic indefinitely, but there was no point to it. If he followed his machine instincts, he would never reach a decision. He had been given conflicting orders, and there was no way to untangle them.

Go with instinct. Go with the tug inside you. Go with what your soul tells you.

Suddenly animated, he scrambled away down the service duct, towards where the Pulse Hammer chamber lay.

Kuikara was clever. Its species had been blessed with an abundance of brain matter, proportionally more than most of the other creatures it shared Deepwater with. This, along with several other factors, had allowed it to occupy a dominant niche in the food chain, out in the unfathomable depths where the monsters lived.

One of the other factors was its size. It was probably half the height of the Machinists' Citadel, with thick tentacles wrapped in a tough, hook-studded, flexible skin that were capable of encircling the massive construction where it tapered towards the top. It was vaguely octopus-like in shape, but its head was stuffed with three rows of vicious teeth, set in a circular pattern in a short, fat maw. Dull grey eyes were set on either side of the mouth, within a shifting pattern of sixteen massive tentacles that were in constant motion all around. Some dragged it along the ground, some probed the air, some swept before it. It was a chaotic, shrieking abomination of black, crusty hide and slick, sheened skin; and it was coming for the Citadel.

Kuikara had not merely headed for the source of the driving pulse of energy along the most direct route, as its companions had done. Instead, it had moved away from its feeding ground, heading further and further around the coast of the Dominions until the sound had become bearable again. Then it headed for where the pulse was strongest, reasoning that it was the source of the discomfort. The pulses were being fired east, to bring the Deepwater creatures across the land. Kuikara approached it from the blind side, from the sea to the west.

When it reached the Citadel, it found thousands upon thousands of tiny land-creatures engaged in battle around it. And as they turned their guns upon it, stinging it like bees, it became angry. And the slaughter began.

The Keriags and the Kuikara arrived at almost the same time. On one side, Macaan's troops faced the immense, terrifying spectacle of the Deepwater monster, blocking out the horizon, its ceaselessly moving tentacles swiping here and there and smashing anything they came across as though they were swatting ants. On the other side, there was the dark tide of Keriags, infinite in number, swarming and slashing with their *gaer bolga*.

The sight of the Kuikara was enough for most of them. Being sandwiched between that and the lethal blades of the Keriags sealed it. Macaan's troops collapsed into a rout, losing all organization, running in any direction that was clear. They abandoned their posts and fled across the fens or into the shelter of the valleys. The Parakkan forces let them go, facing the greater threat that was looming over them. But though thousands of Macaan's troops had deserted, at least as many again remained to make their task difficult. And so the battle degenerated into a three-sided free-for-all between Parakka, Macaan's troops and the Kuikara. Artillery battered at the great beast as it shook the earth with the force of its blows, smashing its hooked tentacles down on gun outposts and sweeping away many dozens of warriors in one go. Wyverns of both sides flew around it, staying out of range of its rubbery limbs, alternately attacking the creature below and dogfighting with each other. Men and women screamed and died in the crossfire, unable to pick their targets as both Macaan's forces and the Parakkans melded into one, their power structure collapsing under the Kuikara's assault.

And all the time, the Kuikara was advancing on the Machinists' Citadel, crawling and sliding across the fens. History would later record it as one of war's ironies, that the Parakkans – who had been fighting desperately to gain the Citadel – had been forced to defend it instead from the vast, black thing that came from the west. For while they only wanted to occupy it to gain control of the Pulse Hammer, the Kuikara was intent on destruction; and the Citadel was the repository of all the technological knowledge in both worlds. Without it, civilization would grind to a halt.

If the Citadel was destroyed, then they had lost anyway.

But nothing could stop the Kuikara.

5

A Game for his Life

Ryushi secured the last strap of his harness, feeling the blazing sun on his neck, and then patted Araceil's flank and looked across at his brother, his eyes like chips of stone.

Takami lay in his own harness on the back of another bull wyvern, several metres to Ryushi's right. He wore his green armour, his silver mask held in one hand, his long, dark hair worn loose. Sensing Ryushi's gaze on him, he turned to meet it with an arrogant smile.

"You'll die today, little brother," he said. "I hope you know that. Your life . . . for *this.*" He lifted the silken curtain of his hair to reveal the ugly, raw circle of scab that had been his left ear. The best healers in the land had not been able to conceal his disfigurement at the hands of Ryushi.

"No, Takami," Ryushi replied. "*Your* life for Father's."

They were no longer in Osaka Stud. Without any of them even noticing it, their venue had shifted to an area deep in the mountains. Perhaps this place never even existed in reality; it may have been entirely a construct of Macaan's mind. Here in Netherfane, anything was possible for him. Ryushi squinted up at the master of the show, shielding his eyes from the glaring sun. He stood high above them, on a knifelike jut of rock, a tiny figure silhouetted by the sun. Where the others were, he had no idea.

At least Whist got away. Maybe he can bring help. If he bothers.

"What was his price?" said Ryushi scornfully, as Takami fixed the silver mask to his face, the screaming-spirit mask that had meant the death of Ty and Banto. "What did he offer you this time?"

"He didn't need to offer anything," Takami said, tossing his hair and lying close to his wyvern's back, testing the nerve-points on either side of its neck with his fingers. "I was glad of the chance to kill you. And after you, I will face Kia, and kill *her* too."

"You're lying," Ryushi said flatly. "Macaan didn't give you a choice, did he?"

The silver mask of Takami's face angled slowly towards Ryushi, a slice of sun turning one half to blinding brightness. For a moment, he said nothing; then he spoke, slowly: "It makes no difference. If I beat you and Kia, he lets me free. If I lose . . . well . . . I'm sure you'll see to me then."

It was the first concession that Takami had ever made to the possibility that he might lose. Ryushi almost felt sympathy for him then; he had chosen the wrong side, and he knew it now. He was playing a game for his life, utterly at the mercy of Macaan, against the brother who had beaten him twice before. When they had lived on Osaka Stud, Ryushi had suffered under the arrogance and scorn of his elder brother; but in the real world, he had proved to be more than an equal to his sibling.

This was his last, desperate chance to break free from the course he had set himself on. It was life – a *new* life – or death. Given the choice, he

87

would have just run, found himself a place to hide, and forgotten the retribution he owed Ryushi for taking his ear. But Macaan had brought him here, for one last reckoning.

The play couldn't end without a showdown. That just wouldn't be right. And in Macaan's twisted mind, the play was all that was left.

The canyon range before them sweltered in the midday sun, hot, dusty waves of heat rising through the deep, narrow slashes in the rock. Perhaps it really existed in the mountains north of Tusami City; perhaps Macaan had created it himself. But it was here that Takami's fate would be decided: live or die.

Ryushi knew something was wrong. He could feel it somehow. This was not all that it seemed. A duel in the canyons; was this Macaan's revenge? He versus Takami. It wasn't enough. What if he lost? Where was Macaan's pyrrhic victory then? He would merely die. There were worse things.

And as he looked into the glaring mask of his brother's face, he realized that they were both going to die here. And Takami knew that, in his heart. For a fleeting second, that was their bond; and they were brothers once more. But then it was gone, and Ryushi hardened his spirit with the thought of the murders his honourless brother had committed.

"Let's go," he said, and Araceil leaped off with a screech, his immensely muscular hind legs sending them high into the air. For a moment, they hung silhouetted against the sun, four wings outspread in perfect symmetry; and then they fell away, and the chase began. Takami's own mount sprang up, unfolding like a fan, and they blasted along the dusty ground towards where it dropped into the vicious canyon range. Shattered arms of rock loomed before them, counterpointed by endless abyssal chasms and tunnels that weaved through the solid earth.

Just like Fin Jaarek, Ryushi thought, remembering his training missions under the tutelage of Jikkio.

Araceil wheeled skyward, peeling away from Takami, and pulled a long, lazy loop in the sky before corkscrewing into the forbidding arms of the canyon range. The air pressure rocketed, thundering past his ears, as the walls crowded close and cut off his view of Takami, who had chosen a different entrance into the maze.

Forget everything. Forget Macaan, forget Kia, forget Calica. You can't fight against Macaan yet. Jedda was right. But you've got a promise to keep, a promise you made to yourself. Father needs to be avenged. Takami needs to die. Forget everything. Just win.

He and the wyvern were one, united in purpose, their thoughts meshed. They were never closer than when they were flying together, two beings become one unit. The beat of Araceil's blood was echoed in Ryushi's own chest, the roar of the wind racing under the wyvern's wings buoying them both. And he *did* forget, everything draining out of him, focusing down to a single purpose: winning. Whatever came after would come. He would deal with that when it happened. All that was left was the moment.

To the right, came the thought, more an instinct than a sentence from Araceil. The wall on that side fell away and there was Takami, a bolt of green fire searing from his hand towards them.

* * *

But they had anticipated it, diving deeper into the chasm, and it flew harmlessly over them. Araceil swooped upwards again and Ryushi unleashed a force-bolt from his outstretched fist, sending it curving towards the underbelly of Takami's mount; Takami decelerated hard, banking towards them so that he flew overhead, close enough for his wyvern's wingtips to scrape Ryushi's matted hair, and the bolt went wild and smashed into an outcropping.

Ryushi pulled up behind him, trying to get an angle of attack, but Takami was swooping dangerously close to the unforgiving red rock of the chasm, turning into it so that it seemed he must hit . . . and then at the last second, the wall relented and peeled back, opening out into a junction of chasms. Takami's risky move had bought him a lead on his brother, and Ryushi curved in close to the wall to follow him, not willing to let Takami out of his sight even for a—

Araceil screeched and suddenly banked hard right, tearing them away from the canyon wall. *Danger!* screamed every fibre of Ryushi's being in response, and suddenly the canyon wall exploded into ochre flame, a great strip of searing heat that reached out to consume them. But Araceil's move had meant they were only hit by the edge of the blast, and Ryushi's shields absorbed the energy.

Careful, he thought. *He might not be Bonded, but he's a good flyer. And he's out to win, too.*

Takami's trick had put him some distance ahead, so Ryushi spurred Araceil into a sharp acceleration. If he lost sight of his target, he allowed Takami the chance of springing a surprise attack. Up ahead was another junction, a dense spray of rocks as if two rampaging canyons had smashed headlong into each other, splintering their stony bones. The walls leaned in close, too close for Ryushi to spare the concentration to throw a force-bolt, and he crouched low to Araceil's back as the wyvern raced to catch up with Takami.

Then Takami banked again, swerving unpredictably, darting into a patch of shadow to his left. Once more it seemed as if he was going to hit the wall, but the darkness swallowed him and Ryushi realized he had found a break in the rock, leading through to an adjacent canyon.

Follow him? came Araceil's query.

No, Ryushi thought. He wasn't insane enough to follow Takami through a tight gap like that, especially after what his brother had just pulled. He'd be waiting on the other side with a fireball, and even Ryushi doubted he could deflect a direct hit enough to stop them swerving into a wall.

But then Takami was back, weaving silently through another, lower gap in the shadow. He had sewn in and out of the wall like a needle drawing a stitch, coming up beneath Ryushi. The Parakkan was entirely oblivious to the danger rushing up at him from beneath, his eyes still fixed on the hole where his brother had disappeared, where—

"Ryushi! Bank right!"

He did so before he had even established who the voice belonged to, pulling Araceil into a barrel roll a second before a gout of green fire shrieked past him, scorching Araceil's armoured underbelly and wings. The wyvern screeched in surprise and pain. Takami cried an oath from beneath him, angry that he had been foiled by. . .

Kia.

There she was, swooping along the canyon on a nimble female wyvern, racing to Ryushi's aid, her short-cropped red hair rippling madly in the wind.

"No!" Takami cried, turning his wyvern sharply and plunging back towards the gap in the shadow from where he had emerged. He saw then the plan that Macaan had in mind for him. This was no grudge match between brothers. The King had told him that he would face them one at a time, not both together. Macaan did not want Takami to win. He wanted the pleasure of finishing Banto's twins himself.

Takami was the entertainment. He was the one who was supposed to lose.

"Takami!" Kia howled, a raw edge to her voice that bespoke the hatred she felt for him. Her stones blazed the colour of magma beneath her tough travel clothes, and the gap that Takami was making for suddenly began to shrink in on itself,

diminishing like an iris lock with a terrible grating of rock.

Takami gritted his teeth behind his mask and dug his fingers into the nerve-points on his wyvern. Like a bolt it flew, tucking its large hind wings close to its body, steering with its smaller forewings; and Takami hugged tight to it as it blasted through the gap a fraction of an instant before it closed. Kia swore, sending her wyvern into a steep climb to crest the top of the canyon and get an angle on her fleeing brother.

Then the landslide began.

At least, it *looked* like a landslide. And it sounded like one; the noise of rock churning over rock was deafening, a grinding roar punctuated by spine-jarring cracks and crunches. But after a moment of panic, the twins saw that the rocks were not falling. No, rather they were *joining*, building, rolling on top of each other to form a canopy over the canyon. They watched in disbelief as a ceiling began to take shape, a great domed mass of boulders that reached from one edge of their narrow sky to the other, whittling the sunlight down to a narrow slash before closing it off entirely with a final, shuddering bellow.

And then all was silence. Only the faint whisper of the wind as they glided, as if hanging in space, looking up at the cracked webwork of bright sunlight that forced its way through the edges of the boulders, providing a faint illumination that penetrated perhaps halfway down the canyon before giving up to total darkness.

In this place, Macaan could do anything. The laws of physics did not apply.

Macaan didn't want any cheating. He wanted them in the canyon, like rats in a maze.

Ryushi looked at his sister, who looked back at him silently, and their gazes said the same thing.

How are we supposed to get out of this one?

"Kia! Watch it!" Ryushi cried, and beneath him he saw Kia pull up sharply, just in time to avoid being speared by a shiver of huge spikes that suddenly ripped out of the canyon wall and stabbed at her. Ryushi's attention being on his sister, it was only Araceil that noticed the jet of boiling geyser water that plumed out towards them from below; he curved away from it with a screech as it scalded the air.

Macaan was having a game with them.

At first it was hardly noticeable: a stone falling from the roof just as they passed beneath, a rock crow cawing out of nowhere to flap at them. Nothing to suggest that Macaan intended anything more than to keep them in his maze with his impossible canopy of boulders. But then it got worse, and worse, and soon they had forgotten all about Takami and were forced to devote their entire concentration merely to staying alive.

The canyons had reduced to knife-slashes, narrow and incredibly deep, with so little light that they were forced to fly with the spidercrack sunshine of the boulder roof skimming uncomfortably close to their heads. Soon the real fun had started. The very canyons themselves had become the enemy, throwing up obstacles in their way as fast as they could handle them. Rocky juts suddenly flung themselves out into their path. Spikes waited for them if they got too near the walls. Steam jets belched up, seeking to burn them with murderously hot water. It was a hectic nightmare, and Macaan was allowing them no respite.

"*There!*" Kia shrieked, and a green fireball came streaking up from the black depths towards her. Not Macaan, this time. Takami. She pulled her wyvern aside, but it was almost too late. Not being Bonded with her mount, she did not have the reaction speed that Ryushi and Araceil had. The bolt seared past as she banked too hard, sweeping towards the steep, rocky side of the canyon. Ryushi caught his breath in horror as he saw that she would not be able to pull out of her turn before she hit. . . . But she gritted her teeth, jabbed her fingertips into the wyvern's nerve-points and urged it viciously round, flipping it over so that its wings caught an updraft from the geyser that had just missed Ryushi. Its belly scraped the rock as it flew parallel to the wall for a moment, and then they were away and safe.

But where was Takami?

Araceil's screech alerted Ryushi to the bolt

tearing up from directly beneath him. *Not this time, Takami*, he thought, and wrenched Araceil into a steep loop. His head went light as he went upside down, the roof of the canyon turning into the floor, and only his link with Araceil keeping him conscious as he pushed Gs greater than he should have been able to take. The bolt smashed into the boulders of the canopy, blowing a great hole of sunlight in the darkness and brightening the interior of the maze enough to see the silhouette of Takami's wyvern below.

The power was already building in Ryushi's stones as he came out of his curve in a vertical plunge. Takami was aghast with disbelief as he saw the manouevre his brother had just pulled; he had not thought it possible to make a loop that tight without passing out, and he was not prepared for the force-bolt that shrieked from Ryushi's outstretched hand as he dived. Too late to dodge, Takami slammed up his defences, taking his brother's blast full-on. Ordinarily, he would have been able to absorb the blast enough to make it harmless, but there was one other factor here. He was flying. And while the bolt did not actually hurt either him or his wyvern, it did send them spiralling aside.

Takami cried out as his wyvern struggled to regain control, its four wings flapping uselessly in an attempt to level out. Above him, Kia had joined Ryushi in a headlong dive towards him. Ryushi had slowed a little, waiting to see what the result of Takami's spiral would be; but Kia was belting towards him at full speed. If Takami had been close enough, he would have seen a spasm of doubt cross his brother's face. Ryushi had been so wrapped up in *getting* Takami that he had not been prepared for the sudden cold rush of dread as he thought that he might have actually killed his brother.

It was an unwelcome hesitation that Kia did not share. She shrieked her hate as she tore down towards him. Nothing could dull the anger she felt towards Macaan and Takami for the hurt they had visited on her. Not time, not amnesia or imprisonment or even the burgeoning love she felt for Jedda. The pain and anger had seemed to die several times over the last two years, leaving her calm and happy; but it was only dormant inside her, waiting for the chance to emerge again at the sight of her adversaries.

And now, as she saw Takami, all the rage she had felt for Ty's death and her father's murder raced through her veins like a living thing and took control of her.

Takami rammed his fingers deep into the nerve clusters at the base of his wyvern's neck in a last, desperate attempt to level it out. The move seemed finally to get the wyvern's wings into sync, and it pulled up.

Right into the canyon wall.

Takami screamed behind his mask, his arms flying up in front of his face as if he could somehow shield himself from the sheer rock wall that they were about to hit.

But nothing happened.

It took him only a fraction of a second to recover. There was no wall there anymore, but a tunnel, a circular borehole, ragged with stalactites, drilled deep into the rock. He pushed the wyvern into a swoop to avoid an arm of stone that spanned the tunnel like a bridge.

He should have hit the wall. He should have

been dead. But that wasn't enough for Macaan. The King had created this tunnel to prolong the chase; he was inventing the landscape as they went.

Takami swore the most foul oath he could, and cursed the day he had ever sacrificed his honour and his family for power and land.

"Kia! Don't go down there!" Ryushi cried, pulling Araceil up into a glide. He had seen the mouth in the rock gape open for Takami, and he knew that to follow him down there would be madness. To fly in such a close space would require more skill than Kia had; probably more than *he* had.

But she was streaking past him like a diving hawk, and if she could have heard him she would have ignored him anyway. She decelerated only a little to swoop into the tunnel, and Ryushi's choice was gone. With a silent prayer to his father's spirit, he pushed Araceil back into his dive, and followed his siblings in.

Elani and Li'ain looked up over the still body of Corm at the owner of the voice, even though both knew exactly who – or what – had spoken to them. Standing in the corridor, amid the reek and glisten of the Guardsmen slaughtered by the Jachyra earlier, was a Deliverer. His face covered by a stitched mask of leather, his hair shaved into black strips on an otherwise bald skull, his shoulders wide and piled with furs, his eyes dark and furiously intense. His voice a rasping whisper, hoarse and guttural, as he spoke to the terrified young girl before him.

~*the balance must be restored, young Resonant. what has been done must be undone. your powers are still inside you. but your glimpse of our homeworld has caused you to be afraid of them. your subconscious does not want you to shift again, in case you see Netherfane once more. but you must, young Resonant. you must~*

"I. . . I. . ." Elani said, unable to think of anything to say. She did not know it, but the fact that one of the Deliverers was talking at all outside Netherfane was an indication of how serious they considered the situation.

"Elani, *try*," said Li'ain, laying an urgent hand on her shoulder. Elani flinched away. Li'ain, unperturbed, went on: "Your friends have no chance in there against my father. I am the only one who has the power to stop him. And even then. . ." She looked down at her delicate hands, tanned and becoming travel-worn from the rigours her new identity demanded. "Even then, I doubt that we can win."

"Can't *you* stop him?" Elani asked of the Deliverer.

The Deliverer bowed his head slightly, his eyes shadowed in the dim, flat glow of the overhead striplight. *~we are governed by laws beyond your comprehension. we may not directly intervene. we may take only such action as is necessary to right the imbalance that has been created~*

Elani's eyes shimmered in indecision. She could try, she had to try . . . but she was going to *Netherfane*! Even the word made her heart clench in fright. This time she was not just blinking through it but actually trying to get there. No, it was impossible. No Resonant had done it. She couldn't. . .

~i will guide you~ said the Deliverer, as if sensing what was in her mind. *~a Deliverer may*

create pockets in Netherfane where an untrained mind may go and stay sane. it is simply a matter of determining which physical laws apply. Macaan has done this. i can show you to his domain. i can guide you, but i cannot take you. it is not permitted. only you can do that~

"Please. . ." said Li'ain. "You have to try."

"Whadd*you* care, anyway?" Elani snapped suddenly, turning on her. "You spent half your time trying to kill us all, *Aurin*. You want me to take you back to your father so you can team up with him again? Finish the job?"

Li'ain's face tautened in pain at her words. "I want you. . ." she said quietly. "I want you to take me to Ryushi. And Kia."

"You think Kia doesn't *know?*" Elani cried. "You think she'd want your help? It was your fault that Ty was killed!"

"If I don't go, they'll die," Li'ain whispered, looking at Corm's body. "You can't make me responsible for *their* deaths as well."

Elani looked from her to the Deliverer. The Deliverer gazed back at her steadily. Further down the corridor, footsteps and shouted voices were becoming louder. Guardsmen. The reinforcements were arriving.

~time is short, young Resonant~

"Why does everyone always lay this stuff on *me*?" Elani cried petulantly, then grabbed the Deliverer's hand and Li'ain's, and, before she had time to think better of it, shifted as hard as she could.

It was like something snapped inside. The barrier around her powers fell away, destroyed by her faith in the Deliverer's words. She was ten winters old, but possessed of an inner strength belonging to someone three times that age. She had always thought her powers were lost. Now she knew what she had to do, what she had to overcome, it was just a matter of facing up to it. Elani could face up to anything, given the right motivation.

There was a moment when it seemed that nothing was going to happen, that they were going to remain in that bloodied corridor, hands linked in the hot gloom, until the Guardsmen arrived. Then there was a jolt, much rougher than any of Elani's previous efforts, and they were gone.

When the black-armoured soldiers arrived, there was only Corm there, silent and still. They stepped over him without a second glance, punched in the code to open the doors, and went into the Pulse Hammer chamber.

6

No Place for Fear

Tusami City was no more.

Once it had been a bustling metropolis, a sweaty mass of iron and steel populated by a hundred thousand and more. Once its streets had crawled all the way up the face of the mountains that abutted it from behind. Once it was the northernmost city in the Dominions.

Now it was nothing but a ruin, its streets flattened and aflame, thin rivers of red magma picking their way through the blackened rubble and twisted jumbles of metal. Dust from the destruction had thrown up a dour cloud over all, muting the sunlight to gloom and causing the temperature to dip. As if in sympathy, natural clouds were gathering fast from the north, a monumental thunderhead approaching like a colossus.

Much of the populace had taken shelter from the twin attack of Fal Juja and the Mau Grist by hiding in the tunnel system that usually housed the poorest third of the city's denizens. The tunnels cut deep into the mountainside, an underground network of dwellings and markets, surrounded by metres of solid rock. The destruction of the magma derricks had caused a few cave-ins in the older parts of the tunnels, but by and large the people had been protected by the thick stone. Now they carefully picked their way out, emerging at ground level to gaze with slack-jawed horror upon what had become of their homes.

After a time, leaders emerged, men and women who raised their voices above the milling confusion of the people and ordered them to form into search and rescue parties. There were a good many thousand folk who had been out in the open when the blast hit, fighting to defend against the great Deepwater monsters. The survivors owed it to the wounded to make every effort to find them.

And so they began, spreading out across the

wrecked city. Their progress was slow, for the streets – such as they were – had been brutally rearranged, and there were no easy routes across the rubble. Hulking girders loomed over them; thinly covered pitfalls threatened to claim new lives; mini-landslides still fell from the mountain face. Gutted buildings, only their warped metal structures still standing, provided grim and occasionally recognizable landmarks.

The search had been going for an hour or more when the drizzle began, rapidly thickening into rain, and from there to a cloudburst. The dazed and tired rescue teams did up their collars, squared their shoulders and kept going. Seventeen people had already been found, and were being treated back in the tunnels. Ten times that many had been beyond treatment.

The rain whipped and lashed at the ruined city, turning its hot, dusty air to cool wet sheets, running between the haphazard jumbles of broken stone, finding routes through seemingly impassable obstacles, questing downward.

Finding a young Noman boy.

Gerdi awoke, flinching away from the cold

splutter of water that soaked his cheek. For a disorientating second, he was not sure whether his eyes were open or not. The blackness was total, and swarmed with inky shapes. Then he saw the faint, tiny triangle of half-light above him, through which the water splashed and murmured. He fixed on that for a time, re-establishing where he was.

The moment of understanding, when it came, was like being punched in the chest from the inside.

In the close darkness, he scrambled for the glowstone in his pouch and tore off the rag that wrapped it, and then stopped breathing as he saw what it revealed.

He was inside a tomb of rock, a haphazard collection of angles and flat planes that tapered from where he lay, where there was about four feet from floor to broken ceiling, to about a foot and a half at the far end. The thin gurgle of water splashed incessantly down upon him, but he was not even aware of it.

The gazebo had collapsed on them in the blast, its roof protecting them from the rubble of the surrounding buildings. Only the tiny triangle of dull light through which the water came gave them any idea of how deep they were buried.

The others were there. Still, dirty and bloodied. Had he noticed it, he would have seen that he was in a similar state, with one side of his wild green hair plastered down with red moistness and his face and skin coated in a thin film of beige dust. But his eyes were fixed on Hochi, who was lying next to him, his shirt rent by a great slash across his massive chest, soaked dark by blood. His features were still as the stone that surrounded them, bruised and purpled.

Gerdi felt a sob of fright hitch into his throat, and suddenly he felt nothing like he usually did, a cocky kid with a self-confidence that bordered on arrogance. At that moment, he was just a scared fourteen-winter child.

Leaving the glowstone, he scrambled over to Hochi and shook him gently by the shoulders.

"Hey, Hoch?" he prompted, his voice breaking. "Hey, boss-man? You okay? *Hoch?*"

He pressed his fingers to Hochi's throat, finding the carotid artery. For a terrifying few seconds, there was nothing; then he felt it, the faint throb of a pulse. There was still life in the big man's body. But for how much longer?

There was a stirring just beyond him, and he looked up to see Peliqua levering herself upon one elbow, coughing hard enough to retch. Her cream-on-white Kirin eyes fell on him, then down to Hochi, and then went beyond them both. She made a small "oh" noise in the back of her throat and then closed her eyes. Gerdi watched her for a moment and saw a tear squeeze through her lashes, then turned to see what she had seen.

At the widest end of their tiny sliver of space, there was Iriqi, lying on its side, its massive shoulders squeezed together across its thin chest. The Koth Taraan had taken the brunt of the falling gazebo to protect them all. If Iriqi had not been there, the roof would have collapsed entirely.

But the creature's head was lolling, and its huge eyes were glazed pools of black. It was dead, gone to join the Communion which linked its people together.

Lying next to it was Jaan, curled up in the foetal position, his beaded clumps of hair covering his face in a thick veil. Chunks of rubble were strewn all around him. Gerdi crawled over to the Kirin boy, feeling Peliqua's fragile gaze on his back. For a moment, he hesitated; then he brushed aside Jaan's hair and held his fingers to the grey skin of his throat. He sat there in silence for a short while, dreading what he had to do next.

"He's dead, isn't he?" Peliqua whispered.

Above them, a lone rescuer saw the light of the glowstone shining in the rubble, a tiny triangle of brightness in the dull grey. She motioned to her nearby companions, and hurried over to the spot. "Is anybody down there?" she called.

Gerdi began to cry.

From the safety of the service duct, the flat black lenses of Chiro's eyes watched the Guardsmen picking their way among the dead.

The Pulse Hammer room was cluttered with corpses, Jachyra and Guardsmen alike. The Jachyra were by and large unmarked; the fallen Guardsmen were in a considerably worse state.

It was not hard to establish what had happened. Those Guardsmen who walked around, poking through the carnage, were reinforcements, summoned to guard the Pulse Hammer after their predecessors had failed. The King himself had killed the Jachyra after they slaughtered the sentries, using the trigger-stone in his forehead. Reports had been going back and forth across the Citadel that several of Macaan's other high-ranking generals had dropped dead in a similar way. That, certainly, would have been Corm's fate, and the reason why he was dying when he made his last transmission.

Prognosis: the Deepwater creature outside was going to destroy the Citadel. At least that was what Macaan thought. If he could not have it, no one could.

I can stop them, Chiro thought.

So why didn't he?

Because I have a high chance of dying in the attempt.

The Guardsmen were twitchy anyway. The noise of the thing outside attacking the walls was not helping matters, nor was the sight of so many of their dead comrades. They would shoot him as soon as he broke cover.

He was Breed. He had decided his course of action, chosen which master to obey. It was Corm's orders he was following now.

So why didn't he?

Because I am afraid.

That was it. That was the answer. No percentages, no probability arcs, just plain, cold, human fear. No matter how much he wanted to be a machine, he was flesh and blood. And if he was human, that meant he *had* a soul. And he was afraid to die.

But it was *because* he was human that he had to do this. To save the rest of the world. Not because Corm told him to, but because he must. There would be nobody to help him this time. The communication network had failed almost entirely under the assault from outside. A few lucky shots from Artillerists on wyvern-back had taken out most of the transmitter array. So he was alone.

From his fear came courage, and from his courage, action.

Two Guardsmen died before they even knew he was in the room. The second one's neck cracked loud enough as it broke to alert the others who prowled around the base of the massive Pulse Hammer.

He was Breed, and he was fast. But not so fast that he could avoid six Guardsmen firing at him. The force-bolts thumped into his body, knocking him first one way, then the other, and finally sending him sliding across the floor in a heap to slump against the outer wall, still and limp.

Outside, amid the fens and valleys, rain was falling, pounding down on the battlefield as if it could dilute the death that seeped into the ground around the great, dark cone of the Machinists' Citadel. The earth had been churned and blasted by countless weapon impacts and by the enormous, thick tentacles of the Kuikara, and now the rain melted the mud, scabbing over the wounds that the conflict had dealt and turning the fens into swamps and the valleys into little rivers.

For the great creature that loomed over all, the constant barrage of force-cannon fire was like being incessantly stung and bitten by insects.

Though many generals and foot-soldiers on both the Parakkan and the Royalist side had guessed by now that their bolts only enraged the thing further, the chaos meant that any orders to cease fire were either muddled, lost, or ignored by panicking infantry.

There was no organization any more among the humans. The Kuikara had torn ragged swathes out of both armies as they fought to defend the Citadel. Most of the airborne fighters had either destroyed each other or been picked off by the cannons that fired from the Citadel. The chain of command had crumbled. It was every man and woman for themselves, each side alternating between attacking the Kuikara and dealing with their original enemies.

Only the Keriags were as tight-knit as they had always been, controlled as they were by the hive-mind of the Queens. They swarmed up the gargantuan, leathery body of the Deepwater monster, hanging on with dogged persistence, stabbing fruitlessly at it with their *gaer bolga* spears.

But the Kuikara had had enough. Deciding

with its rudimentary intelligence and problem-solving logic that the principal annoyance was the thumping pulse that came from the Pulse Hammer in the Citadel, it chose to ignore the tiny creatures that crawled on its skin and stung it from afar, and make for the thing they were defending.

With a heave like a tidal wave, it lunged forward, its tentacles sweeping the earth before it, crushing soldiers and Keriags as a human might sweep a table clear of crumbs. Unstoppably, it crossed the last of the muddy fens, shrieking in deafening triumph as it wound the first of its rain-slicked tentacles around the side of the Citadel, followed by another and another until it had enough purchase to drag its immense bulk up the side of the conical mass of black iron. Metal howled and buckled beneath it, a creature half as high as the Citadel itself that was applying its entire weight to the structure. A hundred internal explosions and collapses occurred with every flex of its body.

The troops watched in stunned disbelief as it pulled itself up, its short, thick tentacles whirling and probing around it, until it had got enough height to wrap its foremost appendages around the tapering waist of the Citadel.

And there it began to squeeze.

"You know what it is?" asked one of the Guardsmen, his halberd still nervously half-trained on the limp form of Chiro, his voice echoing up the shaft of the Pulse Hammer chamber.

"A Breed, I guess. Sick Machinist toy. They grow 'em in vats. It's playing around with nature, it shouldn't be—"

The Guardsman never got to finish stating his opinion. Chiro's foot lashed out, his Augmented reactions and strength beating the Guardsman's firing response. The bolt from the halberd smashed into the metal floor; Chiro's other foot pistoned out and went through the chestplate of one of the two sentries standing over him. His first victim had barely begun falling before the Breed boy was on his feet, striking out at the second sentry. Surprise and fear had made that one hesitate; it was more than enough time than Chiro needed to kill him.

There was a squeal and a screech of metal from outside as Chiro raced towards the four remaining Guardsmen who were scattered around the vast, dim chamber. The outer walls cracked and punched inward as the Kuikara climbed them. Alarms blared into life, and a mechanized voice began to drone: "EXTERIOR STRUCTURAL DAMAGE. REPAIR TEAMS TO THEIR POSTS. EXTERIOR STRUCTURAL DAMAGE. ALL NON-ESSENTIAL PERSONNEL EVACUATE THE CITADEL."

The thought raised a flicker of ironic humour in Chiro, a sensation so alien to him that at first he did not even realize what it was. Evacuate. Ha. He was a Breed. He was tied to the Citadel with the strings of his life. If he left it, he would die. If it was destroyed, he would die.

All he could do was try and save it.

Time moved slower for Chiro than it did for the Guardsmen, as his Augmentations stimulated glands and nerves to drench his system in adrenalin for combat. He was bleeding internally; he could feel it. The bolts had killed him already, as he knew they would. He had a short time left before his body went past the point where machinery could keep him alive.

It would have to be enough.

Strangely, he felt no fear. Only acceptance. A machine's response. How much of him really *was* human, and how much cold metal? And how much of the muddle in his mind was either? He would never know now. Perhaps it was best that way. He could never be the machine he strove to be, and he could never be wholly human, either. That was the lot of the Breed.

It is my time, he thought, and leaped aside as a force-bolt streaked by his shoulder, seeming to swim through treacle as it passed in slow-motion. He reached the first of the four Guardsmen and grabbed him by the throat, pulling him into the path of his comrade's fire. The armoured body jerked in his grip as it absorbed the bolts meant for him, and then he was throwing the corpse aside and leaping over the carpet of dead Jachyra to hide behind one of the ubiquitous banks of machinery that surrounded the Pulse Hammer in broken, concentric circles.

Shouts of alarm broke out around him, letting

him know where they were. One of them was grief-stricken about killing his friend. Chiro went for that one. His sorrow and anger would cloud his judgement. A very human response.

Sure enough, the ranting Guardsman made straight for the spot where he had gone into hiding. Of course, by then Chiro had already moved several times and had come up behind his would-be assassin. The Guardsman had just enough time to register that his target was not where he was supposed to be before he died.

Two more. Chiro felt a spasm of pain cramp across his stomach with an intensity that took his machine-regulated breath away. The respirator pack set into the flesh of his back was working overtime in response to his body's emergency status. He hoped it would hold out long enough to—

There. A black-armoured foot, just visible around the curve of a semicircular control panel. He crept forward, his Augmentations making him the consummate hunter. After all, he was halfway to being a Jachyra himself. Breed were made for many tasks, principally for maintenance of the

Citadel; but they were also designed to be capable of defending it.

The first of the remaining two Guardsmen made the mistake of standing still too long while he scanned the area, searching for the enemy that had killed his comrades. The second one was wise enough to cover his friend. And as Chiro leaped out, killing his unfortunate prey with one strike that was hard enough to dent plate steel, the second one sighted and fired.

Chiro felt the terrible impact in his back a fraction of a second before the jolt of electricity palsied his muscles. The bolt hit just as he was spinning from the first Guardsman to throw the halberd that he had ripped from his grip. He did not see the halberd spear his enemy, but he heard it in his unAugmented right ear just before the aural sensors in his left one failed.

He lay on the floor, trembling, fighting for breath. His respirator pack had taken a hit. Most of his systems had shorted out with the impact. His ocular sensors had flickered and died, leaving him blind. He was half deaf, and his one good ear whined with blood so loud that he could barely hear the silence that was left behind. His world had gone black, dark and empty. And he was afraid.

No place for fear, he told himself, and his Breed way of thinking reasserted itself, gave him strength. Where his human side was weak, his machine logic was his refuge. Where his machine logic was inflexible, his human side was creative and intuitive.

I am neither human nor machine. I am only Breed. That is all I need to be.

Slowly, he began to crawl, feeling his way across the wet bodies all around him. Blood mixed with the Jachyra's less identifiable fluids and covered hard armour and mummified flesh beneath his hands. He knew where the control panel was. He just had to get there. His breathing was erratic, a series of tiny inhalations and then one huge breath that felt like it would burst his lungs. But he was still calm. He would not panic. He would take the strength from his machine side, and the soul of his humanity, and between them he would keep his equilibrium.

Crawl. Crawl. Endlessly crawling through

darkness. Until finally, what seemed eternal proved not to be, and his hand fell on the cool metal of the central control panel. He levered himself up, his body jerking again in protest, his arms trembling.

Outside, there was a tortured, booming screech, audible like a thunderclap, as the Kuikara wrapped itself around the topmost part of the Citadel and began to squeeze.

Working by touch alone, Chiro entered the code to close and lock the doors, changing the entry settings so that no one except him would be able to open them. He heard the doors hiss shut over the high, piercing shriek of blood in his working ear. That would keep anyone from getting to the Pulse Hammer, at least for long enough so it could do its job.

His hand spidered over the cortex key. For a moment, he entertained the thought of breaking it; but that would only stop the Pulse Hammer, not repel the creature outside. Slowly, going through his memory, he recalled the layout of the control panel. Three switches and a code to accomplish what he needed. The code he could handle; he knew where the keypad was, and he entered it swiftly. But the switches . . . he had to get them right. He felt the lurking rush of unconsciousness at the back of his mind, and knew he had only time for one chance.

The first one he remembered easily.

The second one made him hesitate, but he got it.

The third one was a toss-up between three possibilities.

No time . . . he thought, feeling his respirator finally pack up and fail, and his lungs slow to a halt. *No time to work it out. Make your best choice. Take a risk. Guess.*

He did so, his rapidly numbing fingers flicking clumsily over the switch and pulling it down with him as he fell, down, down, and then away, to whatever lay beyond.

The Machinists had been exceptionally accurate with their calculations concerning the Pulse Hammer's effects on the Deepwater creatures. They had worked out the theoretical frequencies to repel or annoy the great monsters with little biological data on their subjects and only a few small test models of their machine. Had any Machinists been of a mind to observe, they would have been fascinated with what happened to the Kuikara, which was practically on top of the Pulse Hammer when it suddenly leaped to maximum power in the beat between pulses.

If the effect of the Pulse Hammer on Deepwater creatures had already been likened to a human standing next to a magma derrick, then being next to it at maximum power was like being inside an underwater explosion. The shattering concussion upon the Kuikara's massive eardrums burst the sensitive organs, while leaving the humans around it – whose ears were too small to pick up such a low frequency – completely unharmed. Its death shriek, however, was like a hurricane across the battlefield, causing soldiers to drop to their knees with their hands pressed to their heads.

After it tailed away, all was silence, and the battlefield was a frozen tableau as all eyes turned to the great beast that hung around the Citadel, dwarfing them all. Then, slowly, its eyes rolled back up into its head and its tentacles relaxed, and it slid down the side of the Citadel, an avalanche of blubbery flesh and crusted armour that piled into a heap on the muddy earth.

The two sides had no idea how to react for a time. The Keriags decided for them. They swarmed off the dead body of the behemoth, assembling between the scattered remnants of the Parakkan army, becoming the glue that bound them together, reforming them again, filling in the gaps. The shredded remains of the Parakkan wyvern flights joined them, swooping low overhead.

The Keriags' numbers were vast. Macaan's men had been decimated by the battle. There was really no question as to what had to happen next.

One by one and then dozen by dozen, the action spreading like a virus; Macaan's Guardsmen threw down their weapons and gave up. There was no cheer from the Parakkans, only the silent, weary, flat-eyed glaze of their eyes as they recognized their victory.

Corpses were strewn over the valleys and fens

as far as the eye could see, lying amid the blast-pattern of force-cannons or in trampled obscurity. From the sullen sky, the rain scythed down, lashing living and dead alike. There were far, far more of the latter.

7

Back from the Brink

The tunnel was swelteringly hot, lit by some kind of dim glow that was given off through the cracks in the walls, or by the sullen red of lava spumes. The endless rock pressed in on all sides, a long, curving and uneven shaft that stretched ahead of him. Macaan had created a place that, in other circumstances, would have seemed quite roomy; but Ryushi was flying a bull wyvern at full pelt, and the amount of space there was to play with seemed pitifully small.

The King was up to his tricks again. Ryushi plunged under a spray of spikes that suddenly tore from the ceiling and came up in time to avoid a heaving belch of molten lava that tried to catch him from below. Ahead of him, he saw Kia barely scrape by a jut of rock that spanned the tunnel at a diagonal angle. Takami was there, too; hidden behind the curve of one wall.

We're playing his game, Ryushi thought, in one of the few seconds when he had *time* to think. *There has to be a way to stop this.*

He was struggling to keep up with Kia and Takami. Their flying verged on suicidal. Takami was taking terrible risks to stay ahead of his pursuers, and Kia was being forced to match him. And even though Araceil was a faster and better flyer, they were falling behind because Ryushi was unwilling to take the same risks. Kia was blinded by hate. He had seen her like this before. She would not stop until something stopped her.

For Kia, the sight of her elder brother so tantalizingly close was an irresistible pull. Since their fight in the Sidewinder, she had known that a showdown would come, and she was determined that this was to be it. But every time she got near enough for her wyvern to strike at him, he veered away or dived and somehow managed to slip away from her again. She could not spare the concentration to use her spirit-stones, as she had to devote every ounce of attention to swooping around the constant obstacles that Macaan threw at her.

As if on cue, the tunnel suddenly cracked just behind Takami and began to cave in. Kia did not have time for surprise; she could only react. She sent her wyvern into a rolling dive, feeling the hot gust of displaced air as a rock scraped past her at murderous velocity, then jinked right to avoid another, smaller boulder. For a split second, she was terrifyingly aware of the tonnage of rock falling through the air just above her head; but then she was through.

She allowed herself a moment of relief. It was a mistake.

A lava plume roared out of the tunnel wall, a pillar of fire spewing across her path. She let out an involuntary cry of fright, frantically banking her wyvern away from the blinding heat. It was a testament to her lightning reactions that she managed to avoid the actual lava; but the scorching updraft that came from being so close to something so hot sent her wyvern lurching uncontrollably towards the tunnel roof. A brace of stalactites suddenly tore out of the stone to meet her. Instinctively, knowing there was no way to avoid them, she threw out her hand and her spirit-stones jumped into life, shattering the stalactites as she flew through them with a deafening crack. But it was not enough. A rock splinter smashed into her wyvern's head, ricocheting heavily off its armoured skull-mask, and with a shriek it dived to the floor of the tunnel. Kia gripped its nerve-points, trying to make it fly on, but it was refusing to obey. It spread its wings, decelerated unsteadily, and then landed with a thump on a flat platform of rock near the floor of the tunnel.

"What's up with you? He's getting away!" Kia raged, thumping the back of her wyvern. It ignored her, shaking its head repeatedly as if to dislodge something there. Its bony armour had protected its brain from a blow that should have killed it, but it was stunned and disorientated.

Behind her, Ryushi glided over the remnants of the cave-in and slowed to a halt, landing Araceil next to her on the rocky platform. The glow of magma lit one side of his face as he looked at her.

"Get *after* him, you idiot!" she cried.

"Are you okay?" he asked.

"My wyvern took a hit, that's all," she snapped. "I'll be back up in a minute. Go on, *go!*"

"I'll go when I'm ready," Ryushi said calmly. "You, you're staying."

"I'm *what*? Don't choose this moment to get all sage on me, Ryushi. You want Takami as much as I do."

"Listen, Kia," he said, the thick clumps of his lava-red hair casting his features into deep shadow. "This isn't about you or Takami. It's about me. *I'm* the one Macaan wants. He's just using you two."

"What, you think I don't *know* that?" Kia shouted in frustration. "You think I *care*? He's given us a chance to finally get even with Takami. You want to throw that away?"

"Do you actually believe he'd really give us a chance without a catch? Don't be dumb, sis," Ryushi said. A noisy hiss of a nearby steam geyser almost drowned out his words. Finally, given a few moments to think, he began to articulate the thoughts that had been germinating ever since he got into Araceil's harness. "I think I figured it out.

135

He wants me to suffer like he suffered. He wants me to feel what he felt. There's no satisfaction in just killing me. He—"

"Get to the *point*!" Kia cried, thumping her wyvern on the back. It screeched in annoyance and crabstepped, flexing its wings and curling its neck around to scrape the side of its head against the ground, as if trying to scratch an itch.

"He wants you to kill *yourself*!" Ryushi shouted, suddenly angry. He'd had enough of his sister's senseless hate for those who had hurt her. He'd run out of patience with her constant need for vengeance. In that one moment when he thought he'd killed Takami, he had felt a taste of how empty that revenge would be. There would be a reckoning between them, there *had* to be . . . but he was no longer so sure of what he would do when the time came.

She saw some of the feelings in his eyes, and cooled a little. "Go on," she said, the red of her own hair deepened to fiery black by the magma that ran close by.

"Takami thought he would be facing us one at a time. Macaan lied to him. He wants me to kill

Takami. He'd do it himself if it wasn't so much fun watching us do it. But he knows how you feel about Takami; he knows you won't stop until you've caught him." He paused, leaning forward in his harness towards his sister. "Kia, you're not good enough to fly through this tunnel. Sooner or later, you're gonna slip up worse than you just did, and you'll be dead. That's what Macaan wants. He wants you to kill yourself with your own hatred, and he wants me to kill my own brother for the same reason. Then he'll probably kill Calica and Jedda. And when he's put me through as much as he can, he'll kill me too."

Kia gazed at him for a long while, her face showing nothing of what ran beneath it.

"Give it up, sis," he said. "You've been so mad for so long. I thought, after you got together with Ty, that you'd let it go. But you'd just put it aside. You'll never get back at everyone who's hurt you. You can't destroy Macaan's army singlehandedly. This isn't just a war about you, Kia. There's thousands of other people involved too. *I'm* involved. And I don't want to see you die. I don't think Jedda does, either."

137

Kia's wyvern had finally seemed to clear the fog in its head, and it screeched its readiness, arranging itself for launch.

"Don't, Kia," Ryushi said.

"I have to," she replied, and with a great leap, her wyvern took to the air.

Takami had no idea that his siblings had fallen behind. He was too intent on flying. If he had realized, he might have had some foreknowledge of what was to happen.

Macaan wanted to play; there was no sport in letting Takami get such a huge lead that they would never catch him. When the tunnel floor suddenly flattened out and became a searing river of lava, he briefly wondered why Macaan had chosen to create it. But when the constant attacks on him from the walls and ceiling stopped, he knew something was amiss. He looked behind him, his silver mask underlit by fire, and saw nobody there. But he heard the shriek of wyverns as the twins tore down the tunnel behind him.

Macaan had stopped harassing them to let the others catch up.

He wants me dead, Takami thought. *I know that. But at least I can take Ryushi with me. For what he did to me.*

With the thought came an answering throb from the wound where his ear had once been. And then he saw the immense circle of stone, a great platform that rose out of the lava and stood high above it. A cold claw of dread clutched him, as he realized that this was the end. There would be no more running. The purpose of the platform was obvious. It was to be an arena.

Macaan was done playing. It was time for the finale.

And then his world erupted in scalding, hissing pain as steam geysers suddenly filled the tunnel, blasting over him in an unavoidable roar. He screamed as his mask fell free on one side, only just managing to clamp it back on as his wyvern shrieked and plummeted. The creature had taken the brunt of the hit, and the shock had killed it. Takami, strapped to its back in a harness, was a helpless passenger as it angled downward, towards the stone circle of the arena. There were a few moments of nothing but pure pain and terror as the grey circle rushed out of the burning red to meet them, and then they crashed, sliding and thumping and jolting uncontrollably before finally coming to a standstill.

All was silence. Then, slowly and wearily, Takami reached down and undid the straps on his harness. He slid from the back of the dead wyvern, pulling his mask from his head as he did so and throwing it aside with a high, chiming clatter. Clumps of his hair came free with it. One side of his face was badly burned where the steam had hit it, and the hair on that side was falling from his scalp, leaving only tufts. His armour was still hot against his skin. Only shock kept him from succumbing to the agony.

So this was Macaan's way of ensuring I fight. And lose. The thoughts were not sentences, for his mind was too clouded for that; only a bitter instinct.

He dragged himself to the centre of the arena. Reaching over his back, he slid his nodachi free of its scabbard and held it two-handed before him. All rational thought had fled him now. Only pain was left. Pain, and revenge.

It was not long before Kia rounded the corner of the tunnel and came into view. Ryushi was behind her, close on her tail. Takami watched, breathing heavily, his shoulders hunched, as they slowed and landed. His eyes followed them closely as they dismounted and readied their weapons. They walked away from their wyverns, stepping into the centre of the arena, facing him.

For a time, none of them spoke. Ryushi's gaze flicked from the dead wyvern at the other edge of the great stone platform, to his brother's horribly burned face.

"Takami, Kia," Ryushi said at last, looking from one to the other. Surrounded by the blazing red glow of lava, silhouetted in black, they looked like three demons. The air crawled with heat-haze around them. "This is what he wants."

Kia tapped the butt of her bo staff on the ground. She felt the cold flame inside her again, the old hate. She could think of only one way to satisfy that blaze. "This is what *I* want." She lowered her head and looked at Takami. "It's your time to die."

And with that, the battle began. Takami howled, his nodachi igniting in green fire as he ran towards them, searing down in a great arc towards Ryushi. It was met by his brother's blade, backed up by his own spirit-stones, sending a concussive blast across the arena as the swords hit. Takami parried a blow from Kia, turning his blade to slice at her legs; but she jumped the attack, spin-kicking a heel across his maimed face. He staggered backwards, the hate and rage in his eyes mirrored in Kia's, but Ryushi was already on him, throwing a concussion bolt from his fist that Takami's bubble of defence barely managed to knock aside.

He roared again, all sense and reason gone, hacking like a madman at his two siblings as they circled him. But his blows were not as wild as his attitude suggested; Ryushi narrowly ducked a swipe that would have taken his head off, and Kia almost lost a hand before they learned not to underestimate the accuracy of his attacks. Kia responded in kind, her own face ferocious as she smashed into him again and again, now a parry, there a swift jab, sometimes hitting him, sometimes leaving him a gap which he would exploit. Ryushi attacked too, but it seemed that his heart was not fully in it, and the battle was only between Takami and Kia.

Takami had been holding them both off with admirable skill. But with the new viciousness of Kia's attacks, he could not help being driven back. They moved slowly across the arena, the clash and ring of their weapons echoing above the bubble and rumble of the magma all around them. Ryushi felt his skin slicked with sweat, and Kia looked like she was part of a nightmare in the red light, with her face twisted in fury as she battered at Takami. Would the death of Takami bring her peace? He doubted it.

Father, what should I do? Would you want us to kill your son – our brother – to avenge you?

It had been a question that had never occurred to him until a few short minutes ago, before they had entered the tunnel. He had been obsessed with avenging his father's murder, so obsessed that he had never stopped to ask himself what his *father* would want. Banto was a kind and gentle man. If he was honest with himself – and as he fought with his teeth gritted in this surreal dream-world of Macaan's, he had no choice but to be honest – he knew that his father would not demand an eye for an eye. Retribution, perhaps. But to kill him? No.

What should I do? he asked again, and this time there was no reply.

Takami's blows were becoming increasingly desperate as the shock of his recent crash wore off and the pain began to intensify. He and Kia were both tiring fast, fuelled by a hatred that was far beyond anything their bodies could take. Ryushi glanced past Takami, and saw that they were approaching the edge of the arena, where a long drop ended in the roiling lava below.

And in that moment when his attention was away from Takami, his brother struck. He feinted towards Ryushi, causing Kia to reach over to parry for him; but at the last moment, he switched his stance and drove a booted foot up into Kia's jaw. She stumbled back with a loud clack of teeth, her bo staff hanging loose in her hand, and Takami sent a great two-handed strike swinging over his head and down towards her, his blade trailing green fire.

"*No!*" Ryushi cried, and swung his own sword up to meet it, his stones blazing into life, throwing as much power as he could into his blade as it swept up to meet Takami's.

A hair's breadth from Kia's head, the two swords met. Ryushi and Takami howled as their blows met and matched, and then both weapons exploded with a blast of concussion that blew all three of them off their feet, sending them rolling and skidding away across the stone of the arena.

Takami came to rest on the edge, only a few feet away from the drop that would send him to the furnace below. Kia controlled her slide and came back up on her feet, shrieking in fury. Ryushi tried to scramble to his feet, but he could only watch as his sister, further enraged by Takami's attack, raced in with her bo staff to finish off their enemy.

Takami managed to get to his feet and draw a shortblade, but it was too late by then. He and Ryushi had drained themselves considerably in the annihilation of their swords, and he was weary and slow. Kia knocked the shortblade from his grip, smashed the other end of her staff round the side of his head, and then paused for the shortest of seconds as he reeled.

"This is for Father and for Ty," she spat, and jabbed the end of her staff into his jaw, sending him staggering backward to the precipice. He flailed the air, his arms frantically twitching in vain to try and correct the balance. Ryushi shouted something in the background that neither of them understood; for them, there was only the moment, the meeting of their eyes – Takami's wide in horror and sorrow, set in his scarred and disfigured face; Kia's clouded with rage and hatred, the beauty gone that had once been there. He teetered there, on the edge of the arena, hanging above the blazing river of lava that swept by far below.

And then he fell.

And Kia caught him.

Her hand snapped out at the last possible instant, grabbing his wrist and yanking him back from the brink, sending him sprawling towards Ryushi, where he lay still.

Ryushi stared at her in disbelief as she picked up Takami's shortblade from where it had fallen and tossed it to her twin.

"He's yours," she said, turning her back and walking over to the wyverns. "Do what you want."

For a long time, there was silence. Takami got to his knees, but went no further. His head was hung, his burned eye closed and swollen, the remainder of his long black hair hanging over his face. Ryushi did not know how to react. All of his brother's arrogance was gone now, and without it he seemed . . . he seemed *diminished*. Horribly scarred, broken, defeated, he knelt before Ryushi as their father had never done before him, even at his death.

"Why?" Ryushi whispered.

"Better you never understand, little brother," came the reply, and the rasping of his scorched larynx was terrible to hear. "To know me, you'd have to be like me."

"And what are you?"

"I am what I was born to be. This is my fate."

"You—"

"Don't you understand?" Takami croaked, his good eye suddenly bright. "This is how it was all meant to be! Our paths were decided before we were even conceived."

"Takami, you're—"

"Just *listen* to me," he hissed. "Look at what's occurred. Do you really think that Parakka would ever have managed to free *two worlds* from Macaan if I hadn't killed Father? That single incident, that one moment when I . . . when I betrayed you all. My honour was the sacrifice I made to free the worlds."

"You couldn't have known," said Ryushi. "You're . . . you're making excuses for yourself."

"No, little brother, I couldn't have known. I *didn't* know. But I didn't have a *choice*. Don't you see? My spies have told me a lot about what you've done over the last two years. Don't you . . . don't you think some of it is a little *too* coincidental? That Kettin, a petty thief, had stolen an item of Macaan's jewellery instead of saving his *own brother*, just so he could be there on Os Dakar when you arrived? What kind of man would do that?"

"The kind who would kill his own family for—"

"But that's what I *mean*!" Takami said, thumping the ground with his fist and glaring at him from behind the ruined mask of his face. "I was *put here* to *do that*! Just as Kettin was put here to take Macaan's earring, so you could steal it and Calica could learn about the Integration. Just as Whist was meant to betray you into my hands, so you could be taken from me and meet Aurin. Just as the Princess was supposed to fall in love with you so –" he winced, as pain racked his body from his exertions, " – so you could get the heartstone."

"What are you saying?" Ryushi asked. "That someone set this up before we were even born? Arranging everything so that it would fall just so? That's ridiculous."

"No, not . . . not with that level of accuracy," Takami said. "But if something is in your blood, it will come out sooner or later. People . . . born to love each other will meet in the end, one way or another. You had to defeat me . . . maybe you could have done it in my keep back in Maar, but you see . . . we kept on getting brought back together until you did. That's how fate works."

"But this isn't fate you're talking about," Ryushi said.

"No," he said. "It's pre-programmed destiny. It's all about maintaining the balance. You know Macaan is a Deliverer by now? I've known for a long time. And I've talked to him. And he's right . . . he's right. What he said, it all makes sense."

"What does?" Ryushi asked, forgetting the sweat and heat in the cavern, entirely captivated by his brother's words. Almost . . . *believing* them.

"The Deliverers maintain the balance. That's why they helped you defuse the heartstone. But they're not so passive as you think, little brother. All this was meant to be. All this was *set up*." He coughed, and blood flecked his lips. "It's in the *stones*, little brother. They don't just give us the power. They influence our personalities. They make us what we are. They *shape* our *destiny*."

"According to the Deliverers' plan," Ryushi whispered.

"To maintain the balance," Takami repeated, then lowered his head again. "They see all futures. But they choose which ones they want.

They implant the urges in us at our *pah'nu'kah,* for us to fulfil when we are grown. Their patience is limitless. They are our shepherds, little brother. We are the sheep."

Ryushi was silent. Takami spoke into the ground, only barely audible to his brother.

"Do it," he said. "Kill me. It has to be this way."

Ryushi felt a crawling dread seep into him. "I can't," he said. "Kia . . . if Kia can't, then I can't."

Takami rose to his feet, leaping up in sudden anger, his scarred face inches from his brother's. "*Look at me!* What do I have to live for? I don't want your pity, I want your *mercy.* Kill me! I murdered our father! I was . . . I was responsible for the execution of our family! I killed Ty! *I deserve this!*"

"Takami, I can't," Ryushi said, and suddenly he was calm, clear-eyed. "You've done all that, but I can't hate you for it. Not anymore. I thought I could, I thought I *did,* but . . . now I'm here, I realize there's nothing to hate you for. You made me what I am, Takami. What you did made me take the paths I took. You can't second-guess what might have happened if things had been different.

151

If you had never killed Father, I might have fallen from a ladder the next day and be dead by now. There's no way of knowing. But I'm happy how I am. I became this way because of *you*, Takami. That's how it is, and I can't change it. I should thank you for it; I can't *kill* you for it."

"Little brother—" Takami croaked.

"And no matter what you say, Takami," Ryushi continued, his voice rising, "we choose our own destiny. Even if you're right about the Deliverers, we still have the power to overcome our urges, and we still have to take responsibility for what we do."

"Then let me atone. Let me die with honour."

Takami's good eye fell on the blade in Ryushi's hand. Ryushi followed his gaze, and the reluctance in his expression was obvious.

"I won't attack you, little brother," he said, mistaking the source of Ryushi's hesitation. "I want to make it up to Father. What I did."

"He wouldn't want this," Ryushi said, sudden tears pricking at his eyes.

"Ryushi," his brother pleaded. He had never pleaded for anything. "Grant *me* the right to choose."

152

Ryushi took a breath, shuddering as he released it, and handed the shortblade hilt-first to his brother. Takami's ruined face softened as he knelt again.

"You always were the honourable one, Ryushi. You would never break a promise," he said, unlatching the breastplate of his tarnished green armour and letting it fall to the ground with a clatter. He closed his eyes, inverting the sword in his hand. Ryushi did not move, a tear rolling down his cheek, not daring to look away. Someone had to witness his brother's last act.

"Father, look at the man your son has become," Takami rasped hoarsely, and Ryushi did not know which of them he meant. "Forgive me," he said, and with that he plunged the shortblade into his stomach, angling it upwards behind his ribs into his heart. He gasped a breath and slumped forward, falling on the hilt of the sword, there to lie still.

Ryushi dropped to his knees next to his brother, and his body racked with sobs as Kia came to stand behind him, resting a gentle hand on his shoulder.

8

A Star Might Swallow an Asteroid

It was Osaka Stud again, but this time it was not the childhood idyll that they remembered, but the ruin that had been left behind by Macaan's attack, two years ago. The air was dark with curling tendrils of smoke from the crumpled metal circle of the hatchery, and the wheel-shaped stables had only a few twisted girders to indicate where the hub had once been. Jagged triangles of burnt metal were scattered about, some wedged into the splintered trunks of trees, some lying on the ground. The very atmosphere tasted of death and destruction, though mercifully this time Kia and Ryushi had been saved the sight of the corpses of the dead workers. The haze of dust that was kicked up during the real attack had settled, and the sky was clear and blue, a fine summer's day.

Calica threw her arms around Ryushi before he had even established where he was. All he remembered was a sudden wrench, and then the tunnel, the lava, and Takami were all gone, and he was here, blinded by the sun that beamed overhead. Araceil was nowhere to be seen, but Ryushi knew that he had been left behind in the lava tunnel. He was safe for now, but Macaan would undoubtedly deal with him later.

"Ryushi! Kia! You're okay!" Calica cried.

"No," said Kia, her voice darkly cold. "We're not."

Jedda followed her gaze to where Macaan stood, his face set tight in anger.

Ryushi gently pushed Calica aside and moved next to his sister, his own expression hardening.

"You lost, Macaan," he said. "You might have us in your power, you might be able to crush us like insects, but you still lost and you know it. You wanted us to kill Takami, but Takami chose his own end. You can make us all suffer, but you can't bring us down to your level."

Kia threw her bo staff to the ground in front of him. "I'm not going to play your pathetic games,

Macaan. Kill us now if it makes you feel better. I'm through."

Only the soft, warm breeze that blew around them made a noise as the four allies waited amid the destruction of Osaka Stud for their captor's response. The twins, the Rai'kel, and the psychometric who had first cracked the secret of Macaan's mind. Calica's orange-gold hair stirred gently; the sun threw a sheen over Jedda's dark skin; Kia's startlingly green eyes stared unwaveringly into Macaan's pale blue ones; and the red diamond of Ryushi's Bonding-stone glinted in the centre of his forehead.

And the King stood, tall and imposing, his dark cloak gathered around his shoulders, his white hair falling around his beautiful, androgynous features, framing the elliptical purple trigger-stone set above and between his eyes.

"I see," he said. "Then if you will not co-operate, it appears I have no more use for the peripheral players." His gaze turned to Ryushi. "But I still have plans for you."

It was a small movement, a sudden clenching of one elegant hand into a tight fist, but the reaction it provoked was anything but small. Calica and Kia screamed, collapsing to their knees as a ball of white-hot agony suddenly blossomed in their stomachs. Jedda went down as well, his teeth gritted hard to prevent a scream of his own, sweat breaking out across his brow and matting his untrimmed black hair to his cheeks.

"Don't—" Kia grated, as Ryushi whirled round to shout something at Macaan. He looked back at his sister, who was regarding him with a fierce and desperate gaze, wincing against the pain that racked her. "Don't give him the pleasure."

"Yes, do, child of Banto," Macaan said with a cruel smile. "You may think you gain something by your defiance, but you will still grant me the satisfaction of your grief and pain as your loved ones die around you."

Calica. Calica was writhing in a spasm on the ground, doubled over and scrabbling in the dirt as if she was on fire.

Tell him, a voice urged in Ryushi's head. *Make the choice. Aurin, or Calica. Tell him his daughter's still alive. You could buy yourself some time, some—*

I can't, he replied to himself. *If I tell him, he'll find her and kill her after we're dead. She'll be—*

Look at Calica! You can stop it!

No! I won't betray Aurin!

But neither could he stand by and watch, no matter how futile his efforts. With a cry, he unleashed his spirit-stones, a howling blast of force that tore across the ground towards Macaan, raising curling fins of dust behind it. The King laughed, a sound of utter disdain, and held up a hand to catch the bolt as he had before.

The next thing Kia heard was a shattering explosion, and the pain was gone, a bliss more intense than anything she had ever experienced. Gasping for breath and drenched with sweat, she looked up.

Macaan was scrambling to his feet, picking himself up from several metres away, his composure ruined, his face both shocked and consumed by fury.

"Impossible!" he shrieked at Ryushi. *"How could you? This is my world! This is mine!"*

~*not any more*~ came a cracked, gargling

voice from nowhere, and Calica's ears pricked up as she recognized the throaty tones of a Deliverer.

Then they were there, materializing in a wide circle all around them, fading slowly into existence, forty or more of the mysterious beings. All masked, all with the characteristic shaven strips in their black hair. Twenty male and twenty female but almost all indistinguishable from each other.

Macaan glared around the circle, seeing that he was surrounded. "You can't interfere!" he cried, jabbing a finger at one of them. "You must keep the balance!"

~the balance was tipped when you used your Deliverer gifts for your own gain~ came the reply, though it was difficult to tell which one had said it. *~we have worked steadily to right it ever since. it has taken us many years. the heartstone you enslaved the Keriags with, the trigger-stone in your forehead, the stones in your back that you put there yourself . . . all these are abominations, perversions of the power that was given to you by the planet. you have abused your gifts. the balance will only now be righted by your death~*

"Ha! You have not the strength to stop me!" Macaan cried. "Your beliefs forbid you!"

~that is why it has taken so long, Macaan. our work is slow, and subtle. but now the time has come~

"Answer me! You cannot directly intervene, can you?" Macaan demanded. "That is your code."

~you are correct~

"Then you cannot take a hand now! It was you who robbed me of my powers, who allowed this pup to hurt me! You have broken your code!"

Ryushi looked up from where he knelt next to Kia, helping her up as the others got to their feet again. Was it true? *Had* the Deliverers taken his power away?

~untrue~ the speaker said. *~we have merely evened the balance of this conflict. that is our way. you still have your powers, but you no longer have the ability to influence the reality of Netherfane. to you, this world is now as stable and real as it is to your victims. we will see to that~*

"I—" Macaan began, but he was interrupted.

~you chose to try and twist the reality of the

bolt, to catch it. had you simply used your defences, they would have worked. we cannot step in to stop you; but there are more of us, and our power is greater in this place. we will prevent any attempt on your part to change the venue you have chosen for your final conflict~

Macaan hesitated for a moment, then waved the matter away with a dismissive hand. "Your feeble meddling will have no bearing on the outcome. You speak of balance, but these children have no chance of winning against my power. You were always too bound by your own rules. That's why I grew tired of you. And now, for all your talk, these children will still die, and you cannot prevent it."

"That is why they brought *me*, Father," came Li'ain's voice from behind where Ryushi and the others stood, and all eyes were on the newcomer that stepped as if from nowhere into their midst. Elani stood with her, the little Resonant child with her chin set and a look of defiance on her face.

Macaan gaped, utterly stunned. Jedda mouthed "Father?" at Kia, and Kia nodded. Jedda's eyes went wide in astonishment. They moved aside to

161

let Li'ain through, and Elani came to stand by Ryushi, smiling her infectious smile up at him, as if to say: *Hang in there, cousin.* Even amid everything, he could not help smiling back. Calica's gaze bored into Li'ain's back, as she came to a halt a few paces in front of them all, facing her father.

"*Aurin,*" the King breathed, forcing the words through the screen of his amazement.

"It is Li'ain now," she replied, in her most chillingly regal tones. "I'm afraid my change of identity is necessary in my new life. The burden of being your daughter became . . . undesirable."

"I thought you . . . didn't he *kill* you?" Macaan cried, pointing at Ryushi.

"Oh no, Father," Li'ain said, brushing her long, black hair over her shoulder and looking at the Parakkan with a strange expression. "He just broke my heart." She turned away, back to the King. "I had my Jachyra tell you I was dead. Tatterdemalion was mine, you know, like the rest of them. Everything you knew was approved by me."

"Daughter . . . *why?*" Macaan looked like he

had been stabbed, his eyes asking the question more eloquently than his mouth.

"Because of what you made me," she said, her face suddenly becoming cruel and sharp as ice. "Because it took my enemy to make me realize that I was a murderess. Because you made me a Princess. Because I don't want to have to take all the responsibility for what I've done when I can blame some of it on my absent father." Her blue eyes had darkened. "And because I hate you."

The words were like a slap to the King, seeming to shake him out of his confusion. Understanding spread across his face like dusk across the day, and the shock and surprise was erased in favour of a deadly calm.

"Then I have no daughter. My enemies have turned you against me."

"No, Father, you did that all by yourself," said Li'ain.

~your plan has failed, Macaan~ said one of the Deliverers, his scratchy voice resounding suddenly across the ruined dream of the wyvern stud. *~even now, the Pulse Hammer is repelling the remainder of the Deepwater creatures,*

*keeping them from the shores of the Dominions.
your army has fallen to the Parakkans~*

Macaan never took his eyes from his daughter.
"No," he said quietly. "It is a lie."

*~you used to be one of us, Macaan. you know
we do not lie~*

Macaan was silent for a moment. Then a shout
began to build in his throat, starting off as little
more than a purr and growing in intensity,
becoming a howl, a terrible sound of utter
despair, rage and frustration. His head was tipped
to the sky, his fists balled, shaking with the
knowledge of his defeat and loss.

And then, just as his fury reached its
crescendo, he threw his arms forward, unleashing
all his anger in a white-hot inferno of destruction,
a torrent of energy that engulfed everything before
him, swallowing the Parakkans and their allies
like a star might swallow an asteroid.

Elani screamed, holding her hands to her ears,
and Ryushi dropped to one knee and hugged her
into his shoulder. Jedda flinched, staggering
backwards and shielding his eyes. Calica and Kia
faced the power without blinking.

Li'ain's forearms were crossed before her face, her black hair lashing around her as if she stood in the path of a hurricane, leaning forward into the blast. The bubble of energy that encased them all crackled with a seething green and black energy – the power of chaos, disorder. Macaan's attack was disintegrating as it hit the barrier Li'ain had thrown up around them; now it was only she that stood between them and the hellish maelstrom outside.

"Kia! Ryushi!" she cried. "I cannot hold him for long!"

Ryushi got up, hurrying to her side. Kia joined him, and as one they released the power in their stones; Ryushi throwing out his hand and Kia slapping her palm to the ground. An immense shockwave roared along the dusty earth of Osaka Stud, accompanied by a fierce force-bolt, and passed through Li'ain's shield without hindrance, streaking towards the silhouette of Macaan, just visible through the roaring flames.

Their attacks did not get even halfway to their target before they were destroyed, fading away to nothing.

"He's too strong!" Ryushi cried over the bellow of the assault.

Li'ain staggered back, feeling her strength begin to ebb. How long could he keep up this constant assault? Would it be longer than she could hold it off? Calica, Jedda and Elani huddled together behind her, within her failing protection, a tiny bubble in a world of furious death.

"Try again!" cried Kia to her twin.

"It's not good, it won't get to him!"

"Do it *together*!" Elani shouted, her high voice cutting through the tumult.

"And do it fast," Li'ain said under her breath, her muscles beginning to ache. She had more power than almost anyone else in either world, but she still could not beat the one who had given her spirit-stones.

Kia gripped her brother's hand. "Worth a try," she said.

"Let's go, sis," he said. "All we've got." And together they closed their eyes, and reached down deep into themselves.

Nothing happened.

"Come on, come on," Elani whispered under

her breath. "Remember . . . remember what you used to be like. You used to be *twins*, don't you remember? You used to be close."

Ryushi opened his eyes, breathing out with a disappointed hiss of breath. "It's not *working*," he said.

"It *will* work, bro," Kia said. "It's got to. Forget Ty and I'll forget Calica. Forget what we did. You're all the family I've got left, Ryushi. Do it for Father, for Takami, whatever. Just *try*."

He did so. He closed his eyes, shutting out the rapid breathing of Li'ain, ignoring the faint sounds of pain that were coming from her as she struggled to keep her rapidly crumbling defences up. He concentrated only on home, Osaka Stud, in the days before it was destroyed. Isolated, beautiful, they had known no other place but that until the moment when they had fled from their father's death so long ago. He remembered training with Kia, playing with her, before the rage and hate had consumed her. They were twins; they shared everything that they had. They had been inseparable, until the impossible had happened.

He loved her. She was his twin sister, and no matter what had happened between them, he would always love her, even when she was not with him. He had never admitted it to himself before, and with that realization, everything else seemed so ridiculous and petty. All the fights and jealousy they had been through. It didn't matter. Because he loved his sister, and she loved him, and that was all that counted.

The surge of energy that raced through the ground and into their stones was breathtaking in its intensity; it filled them with searing warmth for a second and then burst forth, blasting from their bodies in a great lance of light, parting Macaan's white-hot fire like a veil and arrowing through to the King in an ear-shredding screech of conflicting energies.

The King roared in anger and pain as the bolt hit, smashing into his chest, making him stumble backwards. The twins kept up the relentless blast, pouring all of their strength into a single beam, pulsing and pounding at their enemy with everything they had. For a moment, Macaan's attack faltered, and Li'ain managed to reassemble her shields a little; but then he redoubled his fury, not even sparing a fraction of his power to put up defences, standing up to Kia and Ryushi's attack.

Li'ain's bubble was cracking. The twins threw a last effort into the beam. In the next few seconds, all their fates would be decided. The scales were set: either Macaan would stand up to the twins' attack long enough to break Li'ain's defences, or Li'ain would hold off her father's power long enough for the twins to defeat the King. The circle of Deliverers watched impassively as the match of wills raged.

"I cannot . . . I cannot hold it . . . any more!" Li'ain cried, falling backwards as the last of her power failed.

"Hey, King," said a voice. "Heads up!"

Macaan instinctively looked to the source of the sound, sensing the danger but unable to devote even the tiniest portion of his energy to avert it. He saw the spinning metal disc cutting through the air towards him, and he had only a fraction of a second to realize his mistake before it hit, burying itself crosswise in his forehead, splitting the indigo trigger-stone that was set in his brow.

The world went still. The immense exchange of energies dissipated like smoke in a storm. The twins stared in amazement, their powers drained entirely, only disbelief keeping them on their feet. Macaan turned slowly back to them, his face a mix of puzzlement and horror, the gleaming semicircle of the bladed disc protruding from his smooth, pale skin, the two halves of the broken trigger-stone on either side of the sharp edge.

And then he toppled to his knees, slumped heavily to the ground, and was still.

Whist regarded them blandly from where he stood a few dozen metres away to the right of the fallen King, his dog, as always, by his side.

"You guys wouldn't get *nothin'* done without me," he said. Blink barked in agreement.

10

On the Same Road

In the three months following the death of King
Macaan and the end of what came to be known
as the Integration Wars, both the Dominions and
Kirin Taq experienced a period of rapid change
and readjustment. The Dominions were faced
with the rebuilding of Tusami City and several
other settlements and cities that had been
destroyed by the Deepwater monsters. In this,
they were helped by masses of Kirin volunteers,
who poured through the Ley Warrens to gain a
glimpse of their sister land.

Over a year had gone by since Aurin had been
deposed, and much of the populace of the mirror-
land now knew the truth about the Dominions
and their fair-skinned brethren. The propaganda
and lies perpetrated by the Princess' regime to

keep the worlds isolated and apart had collapsed, and many Kirins felt a sense of kinship with the Dominion-folk, as though they had discovered long-lost siblings. The Dominion-folk were surprised by the willingness of these newcomers to aid them in their time of need, having always thought of them as pirates and murderers. So they worked side by side, and gradually acceptance was gained, and friendships were formed.

The Dominion-folk also had to bear the task of adapting to a new system of government, a democratic council, much the same system as had been implemented in Kirin Taq after the defeat of Princess Aurin. As in that land, the common folk were not overly affected by the change, having never been allowed to participate in politics in their lifetimes. The benefits would be slow in manifesting themselves, but they would come.

The politics and social effects of the new regime is something I will deal with in later chapters. I have chosen to write of this moment because it was here, at this time, that the principal players in the Integration War bowed out and left the stage. Funerals had been held for the dead, *grief and joy had played themselves out, and now they were moving on. Many of them – at least at the time I write this – I have never seen again. But I feel that I will, someday. Fate seems to work like that.*

Excerpt from *Parakka: A History of the Integration*, written by Elani.

The yellow leaves of the nanka trees that surrounded Gar Jenna were turning rust-orange. Nanka trees kept their foliage all year round, but they changed colours with the seasons as regularly as the Glimmer plants of Kirin Taq marked the cycles. It was late autumn now, and soon the leaves would be turning to their wintry red-brown; but Ryushi and Li'ain would not be there to see it.

They stood on a grassy hill on the plains around Gar Jenna, their view of the forest bowl blocked by the horseshoe of mountains that surrounded it. The wind was turning to chill now, and both wore cloaks and sturdy clothes and boots as they stood together, looking out to the horizon. Li'ain's long, fine hair stirred around her elegant, tanned cheeks.

"Where will you go?" Ryushi asked, more from the need to say something than from any real hope of an answer.

"I do not know," Li'ain replied distantly. "Kirin Taq, perhaps. Maybe I will just travel the Dominions for a time. Perhaps I will take to the seas. Who can say?"

A pause. "I wish you weren't leaving," he said.

Li'ain smiled faintly. "And what would you have me do, Ryushi? I said I would not wait for you. Did you not believe me?" She sighed, a light breath. "No, it is better this way."

The phrase hung between them, neither of them needing to elaborate. Calica and Ryushi had become closer and closer since the end of the war, but he had never been able to shovel aside his feelings for Li'ain, the Princess Aurin. Splitlings as the two girls were, he felt an attraction to each of them on a level he could not define. And he could not have both.

Li'ain, like her Splitling, was too proud to be second best. When it became apparent that it was

Calica, not her, who was winning the race for Ryushi's affection, she decided it was time to depart gracefully. Her childhood and adolescence had been spent in palaces and keeps, aloof from the world she ruled. Now she felt a burning urge to explore, to see everything from ground level. The year she had spent under her new identity had given her a taste for experience. She had learned many hard lessons during her travels, and she had more still to learn; but since she had taken on the skin of Li'ain, she found that it suited her well. She, like Kia and Ryushi, had been sheltered as she grew. Now it was time to see what was out there.

"Did I ever thank you, Ryushi?" she said suddenly, turning to look at him questioningly.

"For what?"

"For what you did to me in Fane Aracq. For taking the heartstone from me."

"I can't remember," said Ryushi. "I'd rather you didn't."

"Do not feel guilty," she said. "Had you not done that, I would never have become what I am today."

"I was thinking the same thing about Takami and me. If it weren't for him killing Father. . ."

Her face softened a little in sympathy.

"Too many have died," Ryushi said, his voice strangely thoughtful. "Do you think it was worth it? What would Peliqua think?"

"Peliqua," Li'ain repeated. "How is she coping with Jaan's death?"

"She's strong," Ryushi said. "I can already see her getting her spirits back."

"And you?" she asked, touching the back of his hand with her fingertips.

"With Takami . . . it ended the best way it could. I don't know what would have happened if Kia had killed him. Or me. Kia said that she remembered, at the moment he was about to fall, what the Koth Macquai had shown her in her vision, back before Ty was killed. She said she was just fulfilling the prophecy when she saved him."

"You believe her?"

"No. She forgave him, I think. She got over her need for revenge, just like I did." He was silent for a time, thinking. Then he said: "Takami did what he had to. I'm glad it's ended."

"So am I," she replied, and Ryushi knew she was talking about Macaan. If there was one surviving piece of the cold, cruel Princess she had once been, it had shown itself in the last few months. Never once had she shown any sign of remorse or regret for being instrumental in killing her own father.

There was a snort from behind them, and they looked over their shoulders to see Whist leading a pakpak up the slope, heavily laden with baggage. It seemed odd to see a Kirin creature on Dominion soil, but Ryushi supposed it would become more and more common as the two worlds learned to live with each other. And it was certainly no more odd than the sight of Whist, every inch of his skin covered in swirls and loops of indelible dye beneath a thatch of multi-coloured hair. Usually bare-chested, he was now wearing a long coat against the approaching chill. He raised the hand that wore his armoured glove in greeting, and Blink barked to add his voice to the gesture. Naturally, the dog was with him. Where one went, the other went too.

Ryushi smiled at Li'ain. "And I can't say I approve of your choice of travelling companion."

"Hey, she'll be safer with me than with anyone," Whist said, punching him in the shoulder as he arrived. "Besides, from what I've seen, she can take care of herself alright." He turned to Li'ain. "You good to go?"

"I will catch you up. Give me a moment," she said. Whist gave them an insinuating grin, then wandered away, humming to himself. Blink nudged at them until they petted him a little, then ran to join his master.

"He scares me sometimes," Ryushi said. "It's so easy to forget how lethal he is." He could not help recalling the time in the land-train depot in Maar, when he had murdered a pair of Guardsmen as casually as if he were discarding apple cores. He was an emotionless killer, and not worthy of anyone's trust. And yet, for all that, Li'ain was going with him.

"We are both on the same road," she said, in answer to his unspoken question. "We both need to move on. It suits me to travel with him for now. Who knows what the future may hold?"

"I could never bring myself to thank him," Ryushi said. "For saving us from Macaan. He never told us where he was all that time we were in Netherfane. I guess he winked away the moment we got there, and Macaan never thought to look for him because he assumed he wasn't around. But he never left us."

"He owed my father a debt of revenge," Li'ain said. "It was he who put Whist in Os Dakar in the first place. He is not so forgiving as you and your sister are."

There was silence again. The wind gusted across the plain, rippling the grass. Neither of them knew what to say at their final parting. Then Li'ain stirred, and they held each other for a time, and she kissed him lightly on the lips. No words were needed. She walked away from him without looking back.

It was two days later that Ryushi and Kia rode together for the last time, their horses taking them along a high ridge that overlooked the great harbour town of Yuila. Clouds scattered the sky above the endless sea, and the sun was bright and crisp, lending only a little warmth to the chill wind that blew westward, a promise of the winter to come. Below them, three ships rested at anchor, enormous black creatures of steam and iron that swarmed with activity.

"We really did it, didn't we?" Kia said. She looked better now than she ever had, radiant even in her riding clothes, her short, feathered red hair framing a face that was at last at peace with itself. She had conquered her hate and anger, and it had left her free.

"We really did," he agreed.

"It's stupid, but I feel almost disappointed," she said. "I mean, don't you feel that? Everybody does, I think. That's why we're all leaving. Too many bad memories, too many ghosts . . . those are the reasons we give. But there's nothing else for us to do here anymore."

"We?" Ryushi asked, looking at her askance. "You mean you're going too?"

"To the deserts," she said. "They need me there. The desert-folk and the Sa'arin only made a temporary truce. It'll all go back to how it was before if I'm not there. I'm the only one who can talk to them. The only mediator they've got."

"Now *you're* the one who won't admit your reasons," Ryushi said. "This has got nothing to do with a certain desert warrior, then?"

Kia flushed and smiled. That, too, was another reason why she looked better than ever. She was in love.

"I'm happy for you, sis," Ryushi said, and meant it.

"I'm happy for *you*," she countered. "But I wish we were going together."

"I'll be back," he said. "Someday. I promise." It seemed a pitifully inadequate response, but then neither of them really had the words for what they wanted to say. They had been through so much, and been separated for so long, that they could never be the brother and sister they once were. Their relationship was different now; they no longer depended on one another. It made Ryushi sad that he should have lost something so precious, but it was, in the end, inevitable. Their childhood had been lost in the war, and with it the pure and uncomplicated bonds of kinship.

They had separate paths to follow now, and they both knew it. The moment of severance was too much of a mess of emotion to untangle in sentences.

They rode down to the town below, talking avidly, savouring the suddenly precious minutes of each other's company; and there they rode into the crowds that had gathered, pushing their way through the clusters of people to where the ships waited.

The near-disaster that had almost destroyed the Dominions had one important benefit. The Pulse Hammer prototype worked. Within days, even before the rebuilding of the Machinists' Citadel had begun, the Guild were working on smaller models of the great machine. Less than a month later, the first long-range ship sailed into Deepwater, carrying a mini-Pulse Hammer that would ward away any of the immense creatures that lived there. It returned several weeks later, to near-frantic excitement. Not only had it traversed the sea, but it had found *land*, only a hundred miles to the east.

The fever that the announcement sparked swept the Dominions. People whose homes had been ruined and whose livelihoods had been destroyed by the war clamoured to be among the first to explore this new unknown. They saw a chance at starting again, making themselves afresh. So did Ryushi. He had never asked for any favours in return for his part in the war, although he and his twin were hailed as heroes; but in this case, he made an exception. The explorers were only too glad to have him along.

"Hey, Ryushi," said a voice at his shoulder as he dismounted near the gangplank. "You'd better not get into any trouble out there."

"Gerdi!" he cried, whirling around and hugging the green-haired Noman boy. Gerdi squirmed and pushed him off, glancing around in embarrassment at the milling crowd.

"Ugh! Don't be so sentimental!" he groaned "And don't think you're seeing the last of me, either. I'm on the next ship outta here. You're not gonna hog all the fun. I just gotta hang on for *this* lump of dead weight to sort himself out." He thumbed over his shoulder, and behind him there was Hochi, a broad grin on his face, bandages showing through the gaps in his shirt where they encircled his massive torso.

Ryushi grinned. Hochi had been in a state of recuperation ever since he had been dug out of the rubble of Tusami City. It had been touch-and-go for a month, but he was well on his way to full health now. "You gave us all a scare, Hochi," he said, hugging him gently so as not to agitate his still-healing wounds. "We thought you weren't gonna make it for a while."

"Ah, he was just playing for dramatic tension," Gerdi said. "All that fat came in handy after all, I guess."

"We'll see who's fat when I'm fully recovered," Hochi said mock-menacingly, raising a meaty hand. Gerdi ducked away with a cheeky "See ya!" to Ryushi.

"Are you two really coming out after me?" Ryushi said, over the hubbub of the crowd as the ships loaded up.

"I'm afraid so," Hochi replied in his rumbling bass. "There's no Parakka any more. Your father's organization has served its purpose. Not really much point me sticking around here. I think I'll go where the action is."

"What about Elani?"

"She wants to stay," Hochi replied. "She's got some crazy idea that she's going to write all this down, make a record of everything that happened. I think she's adopted Peliqua as her new cousin. All that time they were imprisoned together, it's only natural. And I think both of them have lost people they need to replace."

"You think she'll do it? She'll be a historian?"

Hochi shrugged. "For a ten-winter girl, she's surprised me so many times. I can't see why not. She's pretty special."

A whistle sounded over the crowd. "They're calling you to board," said Kia, who had dismounted next to them.

Ryushi was about to make his goodbyes, but Hochi coughed into his fist and looked suddenly abashed.

"What's up?" Ryushi asked.

"It's about . . . what happened in the Citadel. With Calica. I'm sorry, Ryushi. I wasn't myself."

Ryushi clasped Hochi's massive hand tightly in

both of his. "I thought you were gonna *die*, Hochi. You think I care about that anymore? I forgave you ages ago."

"Thank you, Ryushi," he said. "And good luck," he added, suddenly smiling broadly. "I'd better go find Gerdi. We'll be watching you leave." It was his tacit way of excusing himself, so that the twins could be alone.

Ryushi stood with his sister while the new explorers and colonists bustled past them and up the gangplank, the two of them an island in the chaos and noise.

"You promised to come back, remember," she said, suddenly dewy-eyed with tears. "You better do it."

"Have I ever broken a promise to you yet?" he asked.

"No," she said. "I guess not." She embraced him, and they stood there for a long while like that, silently, before Kia whispered: "I'm gonna miss you, bro."

"I'm gonna miss you worse," he replied.

She let him go and stepped back. "Take care of yourself."

"And you."

They faltered for a moment, and then Ryushi gave her a sad kind of a smile, and he turned and went up the gangplank, towards the great iron ship that waited to take him away.

He felt Araceil's greeting from the deck of the ship as he stepped on to it. Several riding-wyverns had been brought for scouting purposes, and Ryushi could scarcely go without his Bond-mate.

He could scarcely go without Calica, either, and it was she who was waiting for him at the top. She greeted him with a kiss, and then held something out to him.

"What's that?" he asked. It was concealed in her palm.

"Hochi wanted you to have it," she said, a mischievous glint in her olive eyes. "He was too embarrassed to give it to you himself. Said he didn't need it any more."

She opened her palm, and there was the pendant, the small silver disc that had once belonged to Tochaa. The Kirin Taq sun, with a symbol set in its hollow centre. The symbol that was called *Broken Sky* in an ancient language.

Ryushi took it from her, and looked at it for a long while before slipping it into his pocket. He understood now.

We really did it, he thought to himself, an echo of his sister's words. He was still thinking it as the Banto weighed anchor, and carried him into the unknown.